A Highland Homestead Christmas

Willow Glen Book Two

Juliet McKinley

For those who've lost someone they loved fiercely—
and found themselves again in the places they left behind.

Chapter One

Mharie

Airports always smell like canned air and regret. Add in a healthy dose of jet lag and an aggressively chipper customs agent, and it's the perfect recipe for a migraine and I am the lucky recipient. I clutch my carry-on a little tighter and follow the herd toward baggage claim. The flight from Glasgow wasn't terrible—some bumps, a crying baby, and one very chatty boy named Charlie who kept me occupied all the way across the Atlantic. Sweet lad. Bit of a disaster. But then again, aren't we all?

Duncan, the older gentleman who had the window seat, mainly kept to himself. But when Charlie asked where we were all headed after Austin, the conversation picked up.

"Piper Falls," I said, steady as I could manage. "Small town. Not far from here."

Charlie's grin lit up like it was destiny. "No way. Me too!"

He looked at me as if fate had written us into one of those Netflix holiday specials where strangers meet on a plane and end up kissing under mistletoe before the credits roll. I gave him a polite smile and focused on my water bottle instead.

"My sister Abi emigrated there," he explained. "Heading to hers for the holidays."

"My stepdad passed last week," I murmured, the words heavier than the luggage trundling past on the conveyor belt. "I'm here to settle his estate and plan his funeral."

Saying it out loud knocked the breath out of me.

Henry died three days ago.

Three.

And somehow I'm still breathing around the ache that keeps cracking across my chest.

Charlie's expression softened in that awkward teenage way. Duncan gave me a quiet nod, respectful and gentle. After that, conversation kept to safer waters—Charlie's school stories, Duncan's retirement plans, and me? The redhead from Glencoe already missing Gran's kitchen, the smell of shortbread and peat fire still clinging to memory like it didn't want to let go. But I can't afford to linger there. I've got papers to sign. Animals to feed. Grief to pack into neat boxes until I can shove it deep enough to forget.

Customs drags on forever. The overhead lights buzz, harsh and unkind, and the announcements echo like the inside of a kirk. My jumper clings to my skin, wool suddenly a punishment instead of a comfort. Holiday garlands are draped along the walls, silver tinsel already wilting under fluorescent glare. A Christmas tree near the information desk blinks with fairy lights, but its cheer feels hollow when your chest is cracked open.

By the time we reach the car rental desk, the line snakes nearly to the wall. When we finally get to the counter, the clerk gives me an apologetic smile that says it all before she even opens her mouth.

"Sorry, love. We're out of cars."

Brilliant. Just brilliant.

I step aside, arms folded across my chest. The air is humid and sticky, clinging to my jumper like it's trying to suffocate me. Texas in December is not the sparkling winter wonderland the movies promise. I should have worn cotton. Or armor.

"How in the name of Saint Andrew am I supposed to get there?" I mutter under my breath. "Bloody numpties."

Charlie shifts beside me, rubbing the back of his neck like he's about to suggest something half-daft and hopeful, when a voice slices through the crowd.

"Charlie! Charles!"

We both turn.

A woman, Abi I assume, barrels toward us, pushchair first, expression thunderous and terrified all at once. The wee lass inside—Kaitlyn, I find out later—blinks sleepily, while Charlie freezes like a lad caught with his hand in the biscuit tin.

Abi doesn't even slow down. She hauls him into a hug, bells somewhere on her wrist chiming with the motion, and then smacks him upside the head hard enough I hear the crack.

"Ye stupid bloody eejit!" she snaps, jabbing a finger into his chest. "Do ye have any idea the amount of grief I've had these last twelve hours because of ye?"

Charlie winces. "I—"

"Da, ma, Vicky, Rachel—my phone's been melted. Melted," she hisses. "And for what? So ye can nick da's card and bolt across the Atlantic without telling a single soul where ye were going?"

Duncan and I exchange a look that says, in every language on earth, *should we be here for this?*

I suddenly find the floor very interesting.

Abi shoves her phone into his chest. "ET will call home," she declares. "Now."

Charlie grimaces but does as he's told, stepping away to murmur into the mobile. Abi scrubs a hand over her face, blows out a breath, then turns to Duncan and me with a weary, apologetic smile.

"Sorry about the welcome. Someone scared the crap out of his parents," she says, jerking her chin toward Charlie. "I caught the brunt of their concern, anger, and frustration, so... had to get it off my chest."

"Aye, we figured that. That's the kind of thing my sister would dae," Duncan says with a grin. "My ride is here, so I'm gonna head off. You take care." He nods to Charlie, then pulls me into a quick, surprisingly gentle hug before heading off toward a waiting man holding a placard.

"Ye can take the lass out of Scotland," I say, arching a brow at Abi, "but ye cannae take Scotland out of the lass."

Abi's mouth quirks. "Too right," she replies, chuckling, some of the steam gone from her.

She looks me over, eyes softening. "Where are ye heading, lass?"

"I was going to hire a car to go to Piper Falls," I say. "But they've no cars left to hire out."

Abi sucks in a sharp breath. "Yer heading to Piper Falls as well?" She glances at Charlie, still on the phone, then back to me, a plan already forming judging by her expression. "Well that's easily sorted."

By the time Charlie hands her the phone back, cheeks pale and eyes shadowed, she's made up her mind.

"You," she says, pointing at him, "owe the world a few favors. You can haul the bags. She's coming with us."

His gaze flicks to mine. "Aye," he says quietly. "Course."

And just like that, my plan shifts again. Not what I intended, but nothing about this trip has gone according to plan.

We pile into her car, air-con blasting and Christmas music humming low from the radio. Kaitlyn is already asleep in her car seat, her wee head lolling to the side. Outside, Texas stretches flat and wide, ranch gates draped in twinkle lights and giant inflatable Santas bowing in the wind. It feels surreal—holiday cheer painted over a landscape that evokes memories of Christmases past. Somewhere between the terminal and the open highway, my eyelids drift closed too.

When I wake, Abi's voice is softer, the sharp edges dulled as she scolds Charlie again. I keep my eyes shut, letting the sound wash over me. Her words are sharp, aye, but they're wrapped in something warmer. The kind of fierce love that squeezes around your ribs and makes you ache for what you've lost.

It makes me miss him.

Henry wasn't perfect. Stubborn as the day is long. Quiet to a fault. And utterly hopeless with anything that required a password. But he loved my mum and me. Steady. Constant. Five years ago when my mum died, he didn't try to fill her shoes. He just stayed. He was here. And sometimes, that was enough.

Unlike my biological father who decided children weren't for him and swanned off to places unknown.

By the time Abi turns onto the road that leads to the homestead, the ache in my chest feels like it's carved out a permanent place. She catches my eye in the rearview mirror. "You alright, love?"

I nod, though my smile wobbles. "Aye. Just thinking."

She doesn't push. Charlie hefts my bags when we stop, and Abi gives me a hug that nearly buckles my knees. "Anything you need, you call me. Don't make me hunt you down like I did him."

Somehow, I laugh—genuine, if shaky. "I'll keep that in mind."

They drive off in a plume of dust, and I turn toward the long gravel road stretching ahead. The Texas sun is still high and relentless for December. The mailbox still leans to one side, paint chipped, the red faded from years in the sun. I brush my hand across it, remembering envelopes Henry used to leave there for neighbors—feed bills, letters, a newspaper folded just so.

I shift my bag higher on my shoulder and start the walk. Gravel crunches steadily under my boots, and the heartbeat that rattles through my chest is anything but constant. Every step brings me closer to the porch where Henry always waited, coffee steaming in his hand, Dougal snorting behind the fence like a cantankerous welcome committee. I can almost hear him now: "Don't dawdle, lass."

Home. Sort of.

This is temporary. Just until the papers are signed. Just until the animals are cared for. Just until I can breathe again. I repeat it like a prayer with every step.

But the land hums under my feet, and the weight pressing against my ribs whispers the truth—I'm not sure I believe myself.

By the time the house comes into view, that whisper turns into something louder.

Because the porch?

It's a disaster.

Dougal—the massive ginger coo with more attitude than sense—is standing half on, half off the bottom step, buried knee-deep in what used to be Mama's azalea bed. They're not blooming this time of year—just tough, evergreen foliage clinging on for dear life—but that doesn't stop him. He rips another mouthful of leaves free, chewing with slow, smug satisfaction.

"Dougal," I groan. "Get your hairy arse out of there. Those were Mama's."

He looks me dead in the eye.

And takes another bite.

Two heifers have made it fully onto the porch, one nosing Henry's rocking chair, the other trying to worry the faded welcome mat up with her teeth. The boards creak under their weight, twisting my stomach.

Then comes the real show.

A sudden explosion of squawking erupts from behind the shed. Chickens—every last one of them—burst into the yard, wings flapping, legs churning, chaos incarnate. The door to the coop hangs wide open, swinging gently on its hinges.

I follow the trail of disaster around the side of the barn. The feed-room door is ajar too, yawning open like a guilty secret. Inside, a fifty-pound bag of sweet feed has been split open, grain spilling across the packed dirt in sticky clumps. Big, distinctive hoofprints stamp right through the mess.

I don't need a detective to solve this one.

"Oh, saints preserve me," I mutter. "You've been here five minutes without supervision and staged a full prison break. You were so well behaved for Mr. Whitaker!"

One hen hops up onto the porch railing and stares, beady eyed and judgmental. Another flutters onto the rocking chair. A third pecks at a bit of sweet feed stuck to Dougal's hoof, utterly unconcerned about the fact that he could squash her with one wrong step.

Dougal snorts like *I'm* the unreasonable one in this scenario, swinging his head toward me and scattering a few chewed leaves.

"I leave for a couple of years," I tell him, voice tight and wobbling around the edges, "and the minute I show up, you resurrect your criminal career."

He blinks slowly.

The heaviness in my chest doesn't exactly lift, but it shifts. Makes room for something else. Something that feels suspiciously like the beginning of a life I wasn't planning to stay for.

I blow out a breath, roll my shoulders back, and set my bag down.

"Right then," I say, eyeing the cows, the chickens, the ruined azaleas, and the house that isn't ready to be let go of. "Let's start with you lot."

Dougal snorts again and wanders off the bed, trampling what's left of the shrubs on his way to investigate the rosemary bush by the steps.

Of course he does.

Chapter Two

Mharie

I wake to chaos.

Not gentle morning birdsong, not sunlight through the curtains—

Chaos.

Shrieking chickens. The unmistakable thud-thud-thud of hooves on porch boards. And a deep, satisfied *huff* that could only belong to one creature on this property. I sit up too fast, wince, then shove my feet into my boots and stumble outside in the same pajama bottoms I fell asleep in. And there he is.

Dougal.

Loose.

Again.

"Are ye kidding me?" I groan, pushing open the screen door. He's halfway on the porch, chewing on what remains of the rosemary bush like it personally offended him sometime in the night. Feathers fly around him like a snow globe shaken too hard. The hens are everywhere, running in frantic zigzags, screeching their betrayal.

"Dougal Campbell Sutton," I bark, using every surname I can think of in hopes one of them inspires obedience. "I just put ye away yesterday!"

He flicks an ear as if to say *aye, and you'll do it again.* I grab the rope clipped to his halter. He plants his hooves and refuses to move, which is impressive considering his head is still in the shrub.

"For the love of Saint Brigid," I mutter, bracing my boots and yanking with all the strength my jet-lagged body can muster.

He finally—finally—shifts forward with a grumpy grunt. "*Tha thu na thrioblaid,*" I mutter under my breath. You are trouble.

This time, instead of wrestling him back toward the paddock I steer him toward the barn pen, the small, enclosed stall Henry used to keep him in when he was younger and too mischievous for his own good. I unlatch the heavy sliding door, lead Dougal inside, and shove a bucket of sweet feed under his nose to bribe him.

He follows it like a sinner follows salvation. The moment he's in, I slide the wooden bar across the door and drop the metal latch. Then I add a second latch for good measure.

Then a chain. I lean both elbows on the stall door, panting. "Try that, ye escape artist."

He stares, chews, and looks far too pleased with himself. Once I'm convinced he's secure, though "secure" is relative when it comes to him, I step outside to survey the damage. Chickens are everywhere. One is perched on the porch railing, another in the herb box, two are on the steps arguing loudly over a piece of corn.

"All right, hens," I sigh, pushing loose curls out of my face. "Let's get you back where you belong."

It takes nearly twenty minutes to herd them all back toward the coop. The door hangs open, of course, so I close it firmly and check the hinge twice. Then I walk the fence line, looking for answers. A broken slat. Bent nails. A patch where the wood looks freshly rubbed down. "Of course," I mutter. "Ye didn't go out the gate. Ye went straight through the fence like a woolly wrecking ball."

My arms are trembling by the time the last hen is inside and Dougal is secured. The yard is warm already, the December sun beating down as if determined to remind me that Texas doesn't care about my emotional state one bit. I blow out a shaky breath and turn toward the house. It's been looming behind me, quiet and expectant. I haven't been back in more than two years. Work, school, internships... excuses. At first they were necessary. Then it became a habit. And now...

Now he's gone.

I make my way toward the porch, gravel crunching underfoot. The steps creak the same way they always did, though the paint peels more than I remember. I half expect the screen door to fly open and Henry to shout, "You better not be tracking mud on my clean porch, Mharie Campbell!"

But there's only silence.

His boots are still by the back door. Toes pointed in, laces loose, soles caked in dried dirt. It hits me harder than I expected. Like he might step into them any second and come stomping inside, grumbling about the price of feed or the weather turning wrong. I crouch and touch the toe of one. It's scuffed. Familiar. Real. The bird feeder above the steps is empty, swinging slightly in the breeze. He filled it every morning without fail. Said the birds needed a reason to come back, just as people do. I never understood what he meant until now.

I circle the wraparound porch, trailing my hand along the railing. The wood's warm under my fingers, weathered and smooth in all the same places. There's still a dent in the banister from when I dropped a bale hook over the edge trying to impress him. He never fixed it.

"Adds character," he'd said, sipping his coffee like it wasn't his favorite mug I nearly shattered in the process.

The swing on the far end sways gently. The same cushion sits there, a little faded but intact. And on the table beside it, the newspaper. Still folded. Still waiting.

My throat tightens.

I sink onto the swing, curling my knees up, letting the slats cradle my back. The cushion smells faintly of cedar and dust. This is where he sat every morning, coffee in hand, watching the sun rise over the pasture. When I got older, I started joining him often enough that he began bringing a second mug. He never asked questions. Just passed the cup and let the silence do the talking.

I didn't realize it then, but those mornings... they were everything. Quiet but never empty. Still but never cold. Loved in every way that mattered. A tear slips down my cheek. I wipe it away with the heel of my hand. I'm not here to fall apart. I have work to do. Legal things. Practical things. A flight back to catch in a few weeks.

This is not supposed to be permanent. I have an internship waiting in Scotland with the Rural Heritage and Agricultural Policy Initiative. It took me three years, two degrees, and countless grant applications to get it. People don't just walk away from opportunities like that.

I can't.

Even if this place has always felt more like home than anywhere else. Even if part of me wants to curl up on this swing and stay until the stars come out. Even if I still half expect him to come around the corner, coffee in one hand and a sarcastic remark ready to go.

But he won't.

And I'm not sure if I can do this without him. I head inside to get dressed. No more tears. Not today. Time to get to the *obair-latha*—the day's work. He always called it that when it was time to feed the animals, like turning chores into poetry. The feed room smells like hay, molasses, and old memories. Dust motes swirl in the sunlight slanting through the high window. It's familiar and sacred in a way I wasn't ready for. I fall into the rhythm without thinking. Scoop, pour, carry. Check the water. Scratch behind ears. Curse at stubborn gates. The pigs squeal, the hens gossip, and the goats eye me with suspicion. Some things never change.

I find myself humming—an old lullaby my mother used to sing in Gaelic, something about stars and harvest moons. It catches in my throat when I realize I haven't thought of that song in years.

It takes a few hours, and by the end of it, my shirt sticks to my back, and the ache in my chest has dulled just enough to breathe. My muscles protest every step as I make my way to the small barn office, still cluttered with paperwork, baling twine, and a coffee mug that hasn't been washed since spring.

I find the old livestock logbook on the desk. Its leather cover is cracked, the pages yellowed and dog-eared. We used to write everything in here—births, vet visits, feed schedules, weight checks. Every detail, because he said good stock deserved good records.

The last few pages are rough, scrawled in his handwriting, shakier than I remember. Several animals have been marked for sale, a few with names and contact numbers beside them. Some notes are hopeful—"inquiry from Abilene"—while others are scribbled out like he changed his mind.

One name is underlined. A Highland heifer with a note: "Pending pickup – Willow Glen."

I press my fingers against the page. I remember her now— Nessa.

The tiny red heifer born this past spring, all knobby knees and oversized ears, was a surprise calf from one of Henry's older cows, who wasn't supposed to be breeding anymore. He'd said she was "a stubborn wee blessing," which was his highest compliment for anything with four legs.

Nessa. Henry described her as sweet, skittish, curious. Always slipping her head under his arm for scratches. Still practically a baby.

And now someone's coming for her. I swallow hard. Looks like there will be visitors soon. And this time, it won't be me running off. And then it hits me—the funeral. Not the grief of it, but the work of it.

His will is still folded in my carry-on, dog-eared from where I read it on the plane, hands shaking with every line. Henry laid everything out as neatly as he lived: the pastor to call, the hymns he preferred, and which neighbors to notify because they "always brought something good to the table." He even wrote down the inscription for the marker, clear and straightforward, like he didn't want anyone fussing.

All that's left now is the calling.

A list of numbers on a yellow pad he left by the phone, Pastor Reed, Mrs. Hernandez from the choir, and old Mr. Tillman, who helped him mend fence lines each winter. People who loved him. People who'll expect to hear from me.

My stomach twists.

The funeral has to be soon. By the weekend, at most. Which means today—tonight—I'll need to start making those calls, confirming the choices he already made, pulling together the pieces he took care to leave behind for me. Small comforts disguised as instructions.

I close the logbook, sliding my fingertips over the cracked leather.

"Right then, Henry," I whisper into the quiet barn. "I'll see it done. One call at a time."

Somewhere outside, Dougal bellows like he's offended by the delay. A wry, broken laugh slips out of me.

Aye.

One thing at a time.

Chapter Three

Patrick

By the time I hit the edge of Piper Falls, Texas, I've survived six states, four gas station coffees, two dodgy burritos, and precisely one existential crisis in a Dairy Queen parking lot. The GPS cheerfully tells me I'm ten minutes out. My back tells me I'm seventy years old.

Somewhere in Arkansas, I lost faith in humanity. Somewhere in Tennessee, I remembered I don't even like cows. And yet here I am, fifty hours in, driving a borrowed truck with hay scattered across the back seat and a playlist full of murder podcasts because silence made the "why am I doing this" question too loud.

All this... for a cow.

If she doesn't greet me with a thank-you card and a warm nuzzle, I swear I'll leave her at the first rest stop with a note.

The gravel drive winds past a pasture full of shaggy Highland cattle. One of them—Nessa, I assume—is sprawled under a tree like a spoiled heiress in a fur coat. Nearby, a much larger one with crooked horns and serial-killer eyes is attempting to headbutt a gate latch open.

Fantastic. There's always one.

I park beside a red barn and kill the engine. No one comes out.

"Cool," I mutter. "Kidnap a cow, fall off the grid. Classic."

I'm halfway through the barn door when a voice cuts through the shadows, low, sharp, and unmistakably Scottish.

"If ye drag any more mud into this barn, I'll pelt ye square in the face wi' a bucket."

I freeze.

At the far end of the aisle stands a woman in boots, a worn shirt tied over a white tank, and jeans dusted with hay. She's small but fierce, with red hair braided over one shoulder and hands on her hips like she owns the place—or would die defending it.

"I'm Patrick," I say, lifting my hands. "I'm here for Nessa?"

She eyes me like I might be contagious. "You're early."

"You're Scottish."

"Aye, and you've got eyes. We're off tae a crackin' start."

I blink. "You're the... owner?"

She snorts. "Hardly. The place belonged tae my stepdad. I'm just the unlucky sod left tae sort the whole bloody mess."

She crosses the barn, grabs a clipboard, and gives me a once-over like she's still deciding whether I'm worth the effort. "The cow's no' ready."

"She's not ready?"

"She's moody," she says, as if that clears everything up. "And if I push her, she'll bolt like Dougal did yesterday, and you'll be chasing her through the fields in boots that scream bad decisions."

"Dougal?"

She nods toward the pen behind her. "That big numpty in the corner. Thinks he's clever. He's no'. Just misunderstood, wi' a talent for poor life choices and an arse like a batterin' ram."

I peer inside. The massive Highland cow is chewing on a feed bucket, unbothered, while slowly inching its backside toward the stall gate like it's plotting an escape.

"Jesus."

"Aye," she says with a sigh. "He means well. He just doesnae think things through."

I glance toward the pasture and notice a section of fence sagging like it gave up halfway through the workday. "You know your fence is falling down?"

"Aye. Things keep breakin' lately," she mutters. "The tractor, the boiler, gate hinges, that corner post. Dougal tried tae sit on it like a stool."

"Tough time to be managing a farm alone."

Her mouth twitches, just a flicker of something tired beneath the steel. "Tell me about it." But she shrugs it off like she's used to carrying more than her share.

"You'll stay the night. Nessa's no' leavin' till she's good and ready."

"Do I at least get a bed?"

"There's a guest cabin. No telly. No Wi-Fi. No whinin'."

"This is starting to sound less like a pickup and more like a hostage situation."

"Only if you scream," she says sweetly, already striding away.

I follow her, because what else do you do when the woman in charge of your cow looks like she'd bite if cornered and somehow still smells like hay and something floral?

"This how you treat all your visitors?"

She glances back. "Only the ones who show up early and act like they've never seen a cow wi' opinions."

"What exactly do cows with opinions need before a long drive?"

She stops. "Space. Patience. A handler who doesnae act like a tourist."

I cross my arms. "I grew up on a farm."

"With cattle, aye? Angus or somethin' like that. Explains the dead eyes and the misplaced confidence."

"I didn't realize you'd done a full background check."

"Didn't have tae. One look at ye and I knew. You're the helper friend."

That catches me off guard. "The what?"

"The kind that always gets roped in tae help clean up someone else's disaster. Fetch the cow. Move the furniture. Drive across the country for a cow that looks better in a tuxedo than you do."

My mouth opens. Closes. "Okay. That's... weirdly accurate."

She shrugs. "Lucky guess."

Her smirk is trouble. So is the gleam in her eye. And for a moment, I forget why I'm here.

"I'm Patrick," I repeat, because it's the only thing I can think to say.

She sighs, but it's not unfriendly. "Mharie. Welcome tae Highland Homestead."

Roosters are God's least favorite joke. At least, that's the conclusion I come to when one screams outside the cabin window at—

I check my phone. Five-fifteen. Brilliant.

The cabin is exactly as she promised: four walls, one bed, a quilt that smells faintly of cedar and old stories, and a bathroom sink that squeaks like it's apologizing for existing. But I slept. Hard. Exhaustion does that.

I scrub a hand over my face, groan, and pull on a fresh shirt before stepping outside.

The air hits warm and damp.

Texas winter. More like a sweaty autumn.

And there she is.

Mharie stands in the yard with her arms crossed, red braid messy, boots half-laced, glaring at Dougal like she's debating whether murder is legal in this state. He, in turn, is leaning his entire body weight—and his impressive backside—against a gate he absolutely should not be leaning on.

"Morning," I call out, because I enjoy being ignored first thing in the day.

She cuts me a look. "If he breaks that hinge, I swear I'll sell him for parts."

"Pretty sure that's illegal."

"Pretty sure I dinnae care."

There's something new in her face this morning. The sharp edges are still there—bristly, defensive, exhausted—but softened by something I didn't see yesterday. Loneliness, maybe. Or the weight of being the only one left.

"Need help?" I nod toward Dougal, who has now shifted into a slow, strategic wiggle, testing the latch again.

"Aye, grab the rope. But if he drags ye, don't scream. The neighbors will think I'm murdering a tourist."

"Heard worse."

She snorts, but she hands me the rope anyway. We approach Dougal like two soldiers advancing on an enemy who's technically friendly but also prone to violence.

"He gets out often?" I ask.

"Every day since I've been back. Yesterday, twice." Her jaw tightens. "Henry always kept him in the barn when he got restless. I've tried, but—"

"But it's different now," I finish softly.

She doesn't respond. Doesn't need to.

Together, we loop the rope around the big idiot's neck. He resists exactly once, then decides we aren't worth the drama and plods along toward the barn.

"Good boy," I mutter.

"Don't encourage him," she hisses.

When we get him inside, she slides the bolt into place, checks it twice, then leans her forehead against the stall post for a moment.

Just one heartbeat. Small. Brittle.

Then she straightens. "I appreciate the help." It comes out begrudgingly, like each word had to fight its way through pride and grief to escape.

"I'm here anyway," I say with a shrug. "Might as well be useful."

Her lips twitch. "That why ye drove halfway across America for a cow? To feel useful?"

"Better than feeling replaceable."

The words slip out before I can catch them.

She looks up sharply at that. But instead of prying, she nods once, like she recognizes the shape of that ache.

We move through the morning chores together, a rhythm forming that shouldn't make sense but does. She works fast and precisely. I fall into step beside her without thinking.

At the chicken coop, she curses when three hens sprint between her legs and beeline toward freedom.

"Absolutely not!" she yells, lunging.

Without thinking, I dart left, block the path, and scoop up one feathery escapee with both hands.

Mharie stares at me. I stare back, holding a chicken like it's a football.

Then she laughs. Not a smile—an actual laugh. It cracks something open in her face, something warm and wild and completely unexpected.

"Helper friend," she says smugly.

"Don't start," I warn.

But she's still grinning when she lifts the latch and nudges the last hen back inside.

Sunlight warms the yard. The morning smells like hay and cedar and possibility—or maybe that's just wishful thinking.

When the chores are finally done, she wipes her hands on her jeans.

"Tea?" she asks.

I'm so surprised I almost choke on my own breath. "You're offering?"

"Dinnae be dramatic. You earned it."

I follow her toward the house, boots crunching gravel. She reaches the porch steps first, but instead of going straight inside, she pauses.

Her gaze lifts toward the pasture.

And there she is.

Nessa, tiny ginger fluffball, standing in the middle of the field with her ears perked forward, nose twitching at the morning breeze. Curious. Watchful. A little wobbly still, in that way young calves are, like she's trying to figure out how her legs work.

But there's something else too.

A hesitance.

A searching.

Like she's waiting for someone who isn't coming back.

Mharie's voice goes soft around the edges. "Not yet."

"Not ready?" I ask quietly.

She shakes her head. "Nessa's still... unsettled. She keeps wanderin' the fenceline like she's lookin' for him. If I push her tae load before she settles, she'll panic." A breath. "And I'm no' putting her through that."

Her fingers tighten around the porch railing, knuckles pale beneath the morning sun. "She'll ken when she's ready," she adds, gentler now. "Just... no' today."

I nod. "Then we wait."

Her eyes flick toward me, measured, surprised, grateful in a way she'll never admit aloud.

"Aye," she murmurs. "We wait."

Then she pushes open the screen door. "Tea's inside."

And for reasons I don't want to examine too closely, following her in feels less like killing time and more like staying exactly where I'm needed.

Chapter Four

Mharie

The sun isn't even fully up before the weight of everything hits me square in the chest. I should be eating breakfast. Or fixing fence posts. Or making a plan that doesn't involve crying into my tea like some tragic wee cautionary tale. Instead, I'm standing on the porch with a mug that's gone lukewarm, staring at the pasture like it might start offering advice.

Heavy footsteps crunch across the gravel.

Patrick.

His hair is damp from a quick shower in the guest cabin, his shirt still wrinkled from travel, but he carries himself like a man who's already put in a whole morning's work. Typical farm boy—steady, grounded, impossible to shake.

"Morning," he says, voice rough with sleep.

"Aye," I murmur. "Barely."

He falls into place beside me, leaning his shoulder against the porch post. He doesn't fill the silence. Doesn't crowd me. Just... stands there. Like he's got all the time in the world to wait me out.

"You look like your head's runnin' a marathon," he says quietly.

"Feels like it."

A long, gentle hush settles between us—comforting, not crushing. The kind Henry could sit in for hours.

"I dunno what I'm doin'," I admit finally. "This place... It's everything tae me. It's home. But it's work. Hard work. And Henry—"

My voice cracks. "He made it look easy. Fixing things. Mending things. Keeping it all goin'. I can hear him now, tellin' me tae stop fussin' and get on with it."

Patrick nods, thoughtful. "He sounds like a good man."

"He was," I whisper. "How am I supposed tae fill his shoes?"

"You're not," he says simply. "You're supposed to fill your own."

The words hit deep, right where the fear lives.

"And I don't even know if I'm stayin'," I admit. "I've got Scotland. Uni. My internship. Years of plans that dinnae include this." I gesture at the pasture, house, and the land stretching vast and lonely. "Feels like I'm bein' torn in half."

Patrick looks at me—really looks. Steady. Kind. A little too perceptive. "You don't have to decide today," he says. "Or tomorrow. Or next week. But you also don't have to walk away if it doesn't feel right."

"Easy for you tae say," I mutter. "You're not stuck here alone."

"You're not alone." The certainty in his voice rattles me. Warm. Unshakable.

I swallow hard and look away. "I wish other people believed that half as much as you do."

"They will," he says. "Or I'll make damn sure they do."

Something warm sparks low in my ribs. Too much. Too soon. I step off the porch before I can drown in it. "Well, confidence won't fix the gate hinge. And if I leave Dougal alone for five minutes, he'll decide tae redecorate the barn with his backside."

Patrick smiles. "He does have that look."

"Aye. Menace." I grab the hinge oil from the porch box. "I'll be out front if ye need anything."

"Noted," he says.

As I cross the yard, I feel him watching—not pressing, not claiming.

Just... there.

For the first time since my plane touched down, I don't feel quite so adrift.

The knock at the door is too polite to be friendly.

I wipe my hands on a rag and glance toward the front porch. I'd been in the middle of oiling the gate hinge—again—after Dougal tried headbutting the hay shed like a battering ram. Had the daft beast succeeded, I'd still be outside cursing him instead of bracing for whatever fresh hell has come knocking.

Through the screen, I spot a silver sedan parked just off the gravel. The man waiting on the porch looks like he's melting in the Texas sun—khakis, rolled sleeves, glasses that scream estate law.

Must be the solicitor.

I open the door, tucking a loose curl behind my ear. "You Henry's man?"

He startles, like he wasn't expecting an accent—or maybe not mine. "Yes, ma'am. Mick."

I nod and gesture for him to come inside. The living room is cleaner than it's been in years, mostly because I couldn't sit still last night. Grief makes a woman do strange things—like scrub baseboards until they shine and alphabetize spice jars at two in the morning.

Mick perches on the armchair like it might bite. "I appreciate you making time. I know this isn't easy."

"Nothing about this has been easy," I say flatly. "But let's get on with it."

He nods, clearing his throat. "Henry Sutton's will is fairly straightforward, except one clause that's... open to interpretation. He left the property to his next of kin or 'trusted family steward,' a term that isn't legally defined."

My chest tightens. Trusted family steward. Henry meant something by that. He meant *me*. The thought cuts deep and soft all at once. "You're saying someone could challenge it."

Mick shuffles some papers. "Yes. And someone already has."

Before I can ask who, a heavy knock rattles the door.

Of course.

I open it to Wendell bloody Ray Sutton.

"Look who's back in town," he drawls, stepping inside without permission.

"You weren't invited."

He grins, yellowed teeth flashing. "Didn't realize I needed to be, bein' family and all."

Mick rises, extending a hand. "Mr. Sutton. We were just discussing the will."

"Perfect timing then." Wendell strolls in like he owns the place, ignoring the way my jaw tightens. "See, I figured now's the right time to talk about what's best for the homestead. Henry was my brother. Blood. And while Mharie here's sweet and all, she's not exactly... local."

My fists clench. "I lived here every summer for ten years and any break I wasn't in school. I've lived here longer than you've managed to stay sober, ye miserable dobber."

Wendell's smile falters, but he recovers quick. "Still, you've been gone. People forget. This land needs someone full-time. Someone the town trusts. Someone with real roots."

"You mean someone who wants to sell it off to the first developer that waves a check? Is that why you've got a bloody flyer stickin' out of your pocket?"

He pats his shirt pocket, careless. "Don't know what you're talking about. I'm just thinking of the legacy. This place takes money. Work. You planning to run it from across the ocean while you're off doing... what is it again?"

"Environmental policy," I bite out. "Rural heritage conservation. And at least I'm not trying to cash in on mineral rights, ye sleekit wee bastard."

His eyes narrow, but he smirks. "Paper-pushing nonsense. Sounds real handy when the roof leaks or the tractor dies. Folks round here know I can get things done. Can't say the same for you." He leans closer, breath sour, voice low. "Truth is, this place is wasted on you."

Before I can lunge across the coffee table and throttle him, another voice cuts in.

"She's not doing it alone."

We all turn. Patrick stands in the doorway, shirt damp with sweat, one hand braced on the frame like he's been there a while. His eyes lock on mine, steady and unreadable.

"She's got me."

Wendell squints. "And you are?"

"Patrick Williams," he says. "Fiancé."

The room goes still. My mouth opens but nothing comes out. Fiancé? Patrick strolls in like it's the most natural thing in the world, crossing to stand beside me. Not too close, but close enough that I feel the heat of him. He rests a casual hand on the back of the couch.

Wendell barks a laugh. "Well now. That's a new one."

"Is it?" Patrick asks, voice cool. "We kept it quiet, given the circumstances. Henry knew. Supported it."

My brain scrambles, but my mouth manages, "Aye. That's right." My face burns. I want to throttle him and kiss him in equal measure.

Mick clears his throat. "Well. That... does change things. If you're intending to cohabit and manage the estate jointly, that strengthens your case considerably."

Wendell's eyes narrow. "You two planning to stick around then?"

Patrick smiles like it's a challenge. "We are." The bastard says it like a promise.

Wendell glares between us, but the wind's gone out of his smug little sails. He mutters something foul under his breath and stomps toward the door. "This ain't over," he tosses over his shoulder.

"No," I mutter. "It never is, ye sleekit arse."

The door slams behind him.

Mick gathers his folder in an awkward shuffle, clearly eager to escape the tension. "I'll be in touch once I've drawn up the paperwork," he says quickly before slipping out the door with a polite nod. The sound of his car crunching down the gravel fades, leaving the house much too quiet.

I whirl on Patrick. "Fiancé? Really? Are ye daft?"

He shrugs. "It shut him up."

"You can't just waltz in and declare things like that!"

"It worked."

I glare. "What happens when people start asking questions?"

"Then we give them answers."

"You're impossible."

"You're welcome."

I want to scream. I want to laugh. Instead I sigh. "Fine. Guess we'd better figure out how tae fake a bloody engagement."

Patrick grins. "Thought you'd never ask."

I storm into the kitchen before I strangle him. The kettle is still warm, so I flick the burner and find my tin of Highland Co-op shortbread.

Patrick leans on the counter, watching me like he's not sure if I'll hand him tea or hit him with the tin.

"Do you always feed your fake fiancés cookies and tea after a family skirmish?"

"They're biscuits. And only the ones who don't get punched in the face."

He laughs—low, warm—and something traitorous in my chest squeezes.

I pour tea, slide a mug toward him, and sit.

Silence settles, soft as worn cotton.

"Thank you," I whisper. "Didn't expect you tae jump in like that."

"Didn't like how he talked to you," he says simply. "Or about Henry's land."

"He's a right bawbag."

Patrick cracks a smile. "That's Scottish for asshole, right?"

"Aye. With flair."

He lifts his mug. "To flair. And faking it."

"And to keeping that sleekit eejit off my land long enough tae figure out what the hell I'm doing."

"Hey," he says quietly. "You're doing better than you think."

Something inside me eases, just a little.

"Why'd you really do it?" I ask.

He hesitates then tells me—about Willow Glen, about growing up on a farm with his brothers, about long nights and stubborn livestock and the kind of work that doesn't end just because you're tired. About his job in rural development and wanting to help folks keep their heritage alive.

He understands this life.

 He understands *me* more than he should.

When he finishes, my throat is tight. "You didn't have to tell me all that."

"No," he says softly. "But you needed to hear it."

I stare at him—this steady, infuriating, unexpectedly kind man—and manage a whisper.

"Thank you."

He nods, slow and sure.

And for the first time since Henry died, something inside me feels... held.

Chapter Five

Patrick

The first thing I see when I open my eyes is a pair of horns and a wet snout pushing through the cabin doorway.

"Jesus—hey!"

I jerk upright just as Dougal the menace wedges half his shaggy bulk inside. He has already slobbered all over my boots. My *good* boots. The ones I did not buy for farm work.

"I swear, don't do it, you oversized shag carpet."

I lunge for the leather just before his teeth close around it. We wrestle for a ridiculous moment—me tugging, him grunting—until I finally wrench the boot free.

Dougal blinks at me like *I'm* the unreasonable one, then swings that thick head as if he's debating whether to bowl me straight through the wall.

"Not today."

I plant a hand on his shoulder and shove him backward until he finally, *begrudgingly*, lumbers toward the paddock. I follow, sweating before the sun is even up.

A cow should not be able to smirk, yet somehow, he manages it.

By the time I head toward the house, I'm damp, irritated, and reconsidering every life decision that led me here. My shirt sticks to my back. My boots squelch. My dignity feels optional.

And inside the kitchen, I see her.

Mharie.

Hair tied up. Shoulders tight. Kettle whispering steam like it knows better than to get loud around her today. And all I can think about is that moment yesterday—her on the porch with a mug she wasn't drinking, eyes fixed on the land like it was both a lifeline and a shackle. That moment is what made the word *fiancé* fly out of my mouth. Not chivalry. Not bravado. Not even Wendell. It was the way she whispered that she felt alone.

I step inside quietly, but she still snaps her gaze toward me. She's been pacing, muttering in Gaelic, opening and shutting cabinets with more force than necessary. Grief leaks out of her in restless bursts. I take a seat at the small table. Tea waits for me, steaming and unapologetically strong. She didn't ask how I take it—she just remembered. I sip. It burns all the way down.

"So," I say lightly, "are you going to translate half the stuff you were muttering earlier, or should I assume I'm cursed for three generations?"

Her eyes flash. "Yer lucky I didnae curse yer bollocks off, you absolute muppet."

"I'll take that as a maybe."

Her glare is sharp, but the tiredness beneath it is the real tell. "I should've told ye to shut it," she mutters. "But no. You had tae go all knight-in-shinin' flannel. Big damn hero."

"It worked," I remind her. "The solicitor looked like he witnessed a Christmas miracle."

Her lips twitch despite herself. "Aye. And Wendell looked ready tae choke on his own smugness."

I lean forward, elbows on the table. My voice drops. "I wasn't going to let him talk to you like that. Like you don't have a claim. Like you don't know the land. Like you're just passing through."

She studies me—cautious, thrown. "You barely know me, Patrick."

"Maybe. But I know farms. And I know the people who care about them."

She stiffens. "I never said I cared."

"You didn't have to." I nod toward the window—the pasture, the barn, the fence she checked last night before coming in.

"You walked that line without thinking. You checked every latch twice. You looked at Nessa and knew she wasn't ready just from the way she shifted her weight. Folks who don't belong don't notice things like that."

Her breath catches—soft, surprised.

"And the way you talk about Henry," I add gently. "That's not an obligation. That's devotion. Land knows the difference."

She looks away sharply, throat working. "You really are impossible," she mutters.

"And you're terrifying when you're mad."

She drops into the chair across from me, tapping her fingers against the biscuit tin. "I dinnae know how long I can keep this up."

"You don't need forever," I say. "Just long enough to shut Wendell down and secure the estate."

Her eyes flick up. "No strings?"

"Not unless you want them."

She groans and drops her forehead to the table. "Christ on a crumpet, what have I done?"

"Agreed to be fake engaged to a charming, competent ranch consultant who knows how to fix a hinge."

"You're full of shite."

"Absolutely."

She laughs short, honest and it hits me like a punch in the ribs.

But when it fades, she exhales shakily and looks at the kettle like she's trying not to shatter. "We'll need a story," she murmurs. "Something tidy. Believable."

"Yeah," I say softly. "But not right now."

She blinks, surprised.

"We can sort the details tomorrow. After chores."

A breath leaves her, almost in relief. Almost grief.

"Aye," she says quietly. "Tomorrow."

I nod. "Tomorrow."

The moment stretches—not romantic, not foolish—just human. Just two people standing in the wreckage of a day that took more than it gave. She stands abruptly, clearing her throat.

"Right. If we're doing this, ye're stayin' here, not the cabin; ye cannae be wanderin' about like a stray. Guest room's this way."

I follow her down the narrow hallway lined with photographs—Henry laughing, younger Mharie holding lambs, summers etched in sun and dust. It's a life frozen in snapshots, a history too tender to look at head on. She pushes open the door to a small room with soft light and an old quilt.

"It's no' much," she says.

"It's perfect."

She folds her arms tight. "There's a dresser. Closet's empty. You'll figure it out."

"I usually do."

She shoots me a look that says she knows exactly what I mean. We head outside next. She gives me a brisk tour—feed shed, garden rows, the stubborn greens pushing up through winter soil. She doesn't say she misses Henry. She doesn't have to. Every gesture, every glance toward the fence line says it for her.

We stop near Nessa. The little heifer flicks her ear and watches us approach. "She's lookin' better today," Mharie murmurs. "No' ready yet. But close." There's something soft and hopeful in her face, something that nearly undoes me. Back in the kitchen, she pulls out ingredients.

"You cook?" she asks.

"I do."

Correctly? She doesn't say, but the suspicion is loud. I dice the onion cleanly. She blinks.

"Not bad," she mutters.

We fall into a rhythm—garlic sizzling, chicken searing, her shoulder brushing mine when she reaches for the salt. The space between us warms, dangerous and easy. For a moment, it almost feels real.

She stiffens and clears her throat. "Right. Enough o' that. We cook together, but we're no', this isn't..."

"Of course," I say. "Strictly business."

"Aye. Strict." But her cheeks warm, and my pulse kicks hard.

We eat quietly, the house settling around us in slow, familiar breaths. When she stands to clean up, she pauses—one hand braced on the counter.

"Tomorrow," she says softly, without looking at me. "We start shaping the lie."

"Tomorrow," I echo.

She nods once, sharp and grateful and weary.

And it feels like we're on the same side of something much bigger than either of us meant to start.

Chapter Six

Mharie

I close the bathroom door and brace my hands on the sink until my pulse stops tripping over itself. The mirror is unkind after a day like this. Still, I meet my own eyes anyway and tell myself, *"Quit stallin', kiddo. Day's not gettin' any shorter,"* the way Henry used to when I dragged my feet over chores.

I splash cool water onto my face and braid my hair again, fingers trembling only once. I make a tiny promise not to shake in front of Patrick Williams if I can help it.

I want this land. I want to go home.

Both truths sit like stones in my chest, knocking together every time I breathe.

Scotland is the life I built out of stubbornness and scholarship forms and nights spent in drafty libraries that smelled like dust and ink. This homestead is the life that shaped me before I ever had a say in it. I don't know how to have both without something breaking.

From the kitchen, I hear the quiet clink of crockery and the rush of running water. He moves like he belongs here, which rankles and softens me at the same time. I want him to stomp so I can be properly irritated—but no, he's being annoyingly careful with my things.

Enough skulking.

I open the bathroom door and step into the narrow hallway that carries the late-afternoon light like a ribbon. The house smells of lemon oil and good tea, and for a moment, I see Henry sitting in his chair so clearly I have to blink until he fades.

Looking around the room, I'm struck by how perfect everything looks. The tin of tea is back in its place. The towel is folded. The spoon set exactly where I always leave it. Patrick glances over his shoulder as I enter, not hiding how he scans me for cracks. "You good?"

"Define good," I say, because sarcasm fits easier than honesty.

He huffs a soft laugh. "Not actively cursing me in Gaelic."

"You just cannae hear me thinkin' it."

The kettle is still warm, so I fill it and set it on the burner. The click and low hum tug something ragged inside me into order. Outside, cicadas lift their metallic chorus. December sun here is not winter—just heat with softer teeth. The porch boards will still be warm.

"We need a plan," I say, dragging the notepad toward me. "If we're going to pretend at this engagement, we do it properly. No grandstanding in front of solicitors. No accidental confessions in front of Wendell's pals at the feed store. No touching unless someone is looking."

He doesn't smirk. He nods like I've handed him a work brief. "Copy. We'll need a shared story. Timeline. Habits. Favorite breakfast. What songs do you hum in the truck? Who steals the covers?"

"You snore," I say matter-of-factly. "Terribly."

"That is slander."

"Prove me wrong."

The kettle murmurs. I measure the leaves because ritual steadies the parts nothing else can touch. Two mugs go on the table—an old muscle memory. Henry used to carry out two mugs on mornings when he guessed I might join him on the porch. He never asked. Just made space.

"Alright," I say, handing Patrick the pen. "We met on a heritage farming forum last spring. I posted about rotational grazing and low-water pasture management."

"You posted an essay."

"Concise overview," I lie. "You replied with a longer one."

"I was showing my good side."

"You were showing off," I say, but I note the date. "Messages turned into calls in June. Evenings, since I was six hours ahead and you never sleep like a sane person. We started saving for flights in August. Then Henry died, and since you were coming to Texas anyway for Nessa, we moved it forward."

He watches my hand move across the page. "That tracks."

"You proposed on the back porch at dawn," I add. "Coffee on the table. Bird feeder swinging. You said something daft about wanting a life with a view like mine. I said yes because I was half asleep and too hot to fight."

He exhales, not quite a laugh. "Romantic."

"Painfully."

We fall into a comfortable quiet as we write. I note that I hate cinnamon gum and always steal the corner of toast because the crust is better. He notes that he keeps the radio low because voices keep him company on long drives, and he drinks his coffee black unless it's after midnight. We pretend this is administrative, though something under my ribs shifts.

A truck hums past the end of the lane. I flip to a new page.

"The diner and the feed store. Smile like idiots. Buy too many cookies. Let the gossip mill do the work."

"Let the messengers spread the tale," he says, amused. "Smart."

"Photos," I say. "A few around the house today. Porch. Swing. Yard. Then maybe one or two in town when the lights are lit."

He only says, "Copy," and something about that steady, easy agreement smooths my hackles instead of raising them.

We drink tea and call it a late lunch because grief ruins mealtimes until they all feel the same. He rolls up his sleeves and helps without making a fuss. I resent and appreciate it at the same time.

After we clean up, I tie a scarf over my hair and step onto the porch with two mugs. The boards are warm. A wren chatters from the gutter. The feeder sways like it remembers all the mornings Henry leaned on the rail beside it.

"Stand here," I say, pointing him toward the corner where the light falls softly. "Try to look like you don't hate me."

"I don't hate you." Quiet. Steady. Too true. I look away.

He pulls out his phone. We take the first photos quickly, just to get the stiffness out of my shoulders. I hate pictures—they feel like traps. But in the third shot, I forget to guard my mouth and my laugh escapes. In the fifth, he tilts his head toward me like I've said something private, though I haven't.

It's too gentle. I hand him his phone and stare at the feeder until the tightness eases.

"Enough," I say. "Before I start fussing."

"Understood." No fishing for compliments. Just acceptance. It nearly undoes me.

We loop through the pens to make sure no one's staged an escape. The goats look like revolutionaries. The hens have found something scandalous under the blackberry vine. Dougal shadows us like a bodyguard whose attention can be bought with snacks, nudging my elbow when he wants scratches.

"Ye great gomeril," I murmur, rubbing the spot between his horns. He blinks like royalty.

"At least put him in one shot," Patrick says. "Authenticity."

"In for a penny," I sigh, and we try the swing.

The first picture makes me look like I'm about to bolt. The second is better—my knee angled toward him, his head tilted as if I said something only he could hear. The third catches Dougal's ears at the edge, and Patrick laughs so hard he has to grab the railing.

"There," he says. "Proof we live dangerously."

And I laugh too—bright, startled. Like the house cracked a window and let air in.

We stop before the light turns honey-thick. He sends the best photos to my phone at my request. I tuck my phone away in my pocket and try not to look at the screen again.

"The diner first. Then the feed store. One slow loop around the square."

"I'll wear a good shirt," he promises.

"You have a good shirt?"

"At least two."

"Make it three, and I'll be impressed."

"You're hard to please."

"Aye," I say, and let that be enough.

We walk back toward the kitchen. I check the water at the goat pen, run my fingers over the sticky latch, and add it to my morning list. Patrick studies the hinge and says nothing—already thinking through repairs.

Inside, the house glows with soft afternoon gold. The notepad waits on the table. I jot one final line:

Do not engage Wendell alone.

Patrick reads it and nods once—as if he'd planned to say the same.

"I'll head out to check the gates," he says. "Give you space."

"Shout if Dougal tries anything," I say, because being flippant feels safer than being grateful.

"Copy that," he promises, smiling.

He steps down into the warm light and crosses the yard, easy and sure, like a man who's walked a hundred different fields but somehow fits here. I stand in the doorway until he's out of sight. Only then do my shoulders sag. My phone is heavy with photos I'm not ready to look at. I set it facedown and straighten the sugar jar that doesn't need straightening. Outside, Dougal mutters. The hens murmur their evening gossip. The day tilts toward gold. Soon enough, we'll plant the rumors. Tonight I keep my feet on the ground.

I will not try on any ring just to see if it fits. I will not stand at the porch rail imagining futures I haven't earned.

I will make tea, sit on the swing, and breathe until the tightness eases. The kettle begins its soft whisper. I turn the flame up a fraction. The second mug waits on the shelf—not because I need it, but because hope is a habit I'm not ready to break. I don't have to choose tonight.

Only the next right thing. *Obair-latha*, Henry. Tomorrow, more of it. For now, I pour the water, watch the leaves bloom, and let the quiet settle like balm.

Patrick

Morning hits the homestead in that sideways, too-bright way Texas specializes in—sunlight white as bone, air already warming, the kind of quiet that makes you think anything could be lurking behind the next fence post. I'm halfway down the stairs, rubbing sleep from my eyes, when I hear a scraping sound outside. Metal on wood. Metal on... horn?

"Oh, hell," I mutter, shoving my feet into my boots and stepping into the yard.

And of course—it's him.

Dougal.

The shaggy menace has managed to wedge a dented feed bucket onto one horn. It dangles half-cocked like a lopsided halo if halos were made to torment ranchers. He shakes his head, the bucket clanging with every violent twitch, stomping like the ground offended him personally.

"Christ, Dougal," I say, jogging over. "You trying to concuss yourself or just drive me insane?" He looks at me, huge brown eyes and total innocence and swings the bucket hard enough that I have to duck. It narrowly misses my temple. I reach for the rope dragging under his chin, but he jerks back like I've insulted his entire ancestry. The bucket scrapes down his horn, catches again, and now he's snorting like an angry kettle.

"Stand still, you overgrown mop." I plant my boots and yank. He yanks harder. For a second, we're both skidding through mud beside the trough—him fueled by chaos, me fueled by poor life choices. Sweat breaks down my back. Then, with one good heave, the bucket pops free. It sails through the air, lands with a metallic crack, and sends the hens exploding into feathery outrage.

Dougal blinks at me like *I'm* the one causing problems. "You're welcome," I mutter, wiping my brow. He immediately angles toward the chicken coop.

"Unbelievable." I shoulder him away, re-latch the coop, and kick the bucket well out of reach. My shirt is plastered to me; my boots feel like I've run through molasses. If Adam saw me right now, he'd swear I was rolling in muck for sympathy points. On the way back to the paddock, I spot it: a staple half pulled from the post. Fresh scrape on the wood at hip height.

Not Dougal. He's a battering ram, not a fiddler. My jaw goes tight. I press the staple back in and slam the latch home twice. By the time I reach the porch, Mharie's at the door, eyebrows arched up her forehead.

"Good god, what did ye do, wrestle him for sport?"

"Not sport," I grunt, stepping inside and toeing off my mud-caked boots. "Rescue mission. Bucket on his horn. Nearly took my head off."

She presses her lips together. Fails spectacularly. A breathy laugh escapes. "Serves ye right. Dougal's cleverer than ye give him credit."

"Disagree. That cow's two brain cells short of a salad." But she's smiling. The house feels less hollow for it. I head upstairs to drop my bag properly in the spare room, my room now, at least for the duration of this insane fake engagement and stop short. An old hat sits on the top shelf of the closet. Sweat-darkened brim. Dent in the crown. It hits me harder than I'm ready for.

Feels like trespassing to look. Feels like betrayal not to. "Ask before you borrow," I murmur, a pointless rule, but the kind that anchors you when nothing else does. Back downstairs, the smell of flour and warmth fills the kitchen. Mharie works dough on the counter, sleeves shoved up, hair escaping its braid. Her hands fold and press, steady as breathing.

"That bucket was trying to murder me," I say from the doorway.

"You'll live," she replies without looking up. "The bucket too."

"I disposed of the weapon."

"In the yard?" She nods toward the window. "He'll find it again in an hour."

"I hid it," I insist. "I'm not new."

She hums—doubtful, musical. It does something to my ribs.

"Need anything before I," I jerk a thumb toward the back porch, "make a call?"

"No," she says. "I'm fine." She isn't. But pushing won't help.

Outside, the cedar hangs heavy in the warm air. Cicadas punch the quiet full of static.

Hank answers on the second ring. "Williams. Tell me you didn't wreck another truck."

"Not today. Need a favor."

"That tone means trouble."

"I've got a Highland heifer that needs hauling to Willow Glen. Before Christmas."

A low whistle. "You're serious."

"As a heart attack."

"Why can't *you* bring her?"

I look toward the kitchen window—toward her shadow moving across the sink. "I'm tied up here."

"Tied up or tied down?" he teases. "What's her name?"

"Nessa. The cow."

"Uh-huh. And the woman keeping you put?"

"None of your damn business."

"So definitely my business." He sighs. "I'll call Reuben. If he can't take her, I know someone who can. You owe me a steak."

"Big one. I know."

"Don't screw this up, Pat."

I hang up.

When I step inside, the house smells like something real. Something alive.

"Nessa'll get a ride north," I tell her. "Someone I trust."

Relief softens the line of her shoulders. "Good. That's... good." She covers the dough with a towel, hands lingering on the bowl.

"That's one thing," she adds quietly. Meaning there are twenty more. She's not wrong.

I take a long drink of water, trying to wrestle down the heat still prickling under my collar. When I set the glass aside, she's watching me—arms crossed, chin tilted just enough to remind me this land still answers to her name.

"You planning to fix every fence on the property?" she asks, wary but not sharp.

"Only the ones that need it," I say. "And only if you want the help. I'm not looking to take over."

She studies me, weighing intent. "Henry kept things tidy. I dinnae need ye struttin' in like the place fell apart without you."

"I wouldn't insult him like that," I say quietly. "Or you."

A beat passes, softening, not surrender. "Aye," she murmurs, finally. "If ye saw something off at the east fence, go on and check it. Just... tell me what ye find."

"Deal."

Only then does her gaze drop back to the dough. However, she keeps one ear angled toward me like she hasn't fully decided whether trusting me is foolish or necessary.

"I'll take a look," I add, grabbing my tools.

"Likely Dougal," she mutters.

"Maybe. Maybe not." I cross the pasture with wire and staples. At the trough gate, the staple I fixed earlier pulls loose, as if it's been worried at. Boot-height scrapes mark the post. Someone tested it. Someone looked. I hammer new staples and secure a heavier clip. The gate settles with a solid, satisfied thunk. On the walk back, I detour by the lower shed. The old padlock wiggles too much. The hasp creaks. Age or someone checking it, I don't like either.

Back in the kitchen, the dough has risen in a rounded dome under the towel. Like it's breathing. Mharie stands at the sink, staring out the window as if waiting for something she hopes won't come.

"Fence is good," I say. "We'll need to swap the shed lock next."

She nods without turning. "Aye." That far-off look sits in her eyes—the one grief carves. Too many roads. None pointing home.

"One thing at a time," I say, gently.

She blinks, steadying herself, then scores the loaf and slides it into the oven. Ten minutes later, the smell rises between us—holy, warm, steady.

"You're staring," she murmurs.

"Smells like a house that means to feed you." Her shoulders loosen just slightly.

We eat slowly. Warm bread, butter, chicken fried steak, and fresh field peas surrounded by the kind of quiet that feels honest. She tells me about Henry—his stubbornness, his rituals, his bird feeder philosophy. I listen. Ask two things. Let ten go. She doesn't need fixing. Just witnessing. When the kitchen is restored to order, she stretches her back, rubbing her wrist.

"You put the towel right," she says when I hang it where she likes it.

"I pay attention."

"Aye." Soft as dust settling. "Ye do."

It lands deeper than it should. I step outside and lean against the porch rail. The pasture's gone silver. A chain near the shed rattles once—soft, like a warning. I straighten. Listen.

Nothing.

Inside, she hums that low, curling tune again. Not a song I know. But it threads under my ribs anyway. Tomorrow we'll start spreading the story. Tomorrow we'll face Wendell. Tomorrow I'll find a ring that tells the truth without revealing too much. Tonight I let her humming follow me back up the stairs.

For the first time in a long damn while, I don't feel like running.

Chapter Eight

Mharie

The kitchen smells faintly of toast and tea, the last of yesterday's loaf waiting on the rack beside Henry's jam. I brew a fresh pot and set butter and blackberry jam on the table. The lid sticks, then gives, and the scent is sharp and summer-sweet enough to pinch the back of my eyes.

I should be on a different continent. I should be reviewing my briefing for the Rural Heritage internship, confirming my flight back, and checking train times for Stirling and Inverness. Instead I'm barefoot on warm floorboards, cutting bread that tastes like home and hurts like memory.

Patrick appears in the doorway, hair damp from washing, shirt half tucked like he moved faster than he meant to. He stops for a heartbeat, as if he needs to recalibrate to the sight of me, then crosses to the table.

"You're awake," he says, almost pleased.

"Couldn't sleep." I pass him a slice. "Eat before Dougal remembers mischief exists."

"He's plotting," Patrick says around a grin. "I saw him eyeing the coop at sunrise like a safecracker."

"He can try," I say. "He'll fail." I grimace. "Maybe. It's been a few days; he may come up with a new plan of attack."

We eat in a quiet that isn't empty. The clock ticks. The cows complain about a lack of grain. A wren outside scolds the universe because it can. For a few minutes, we could almost be a couple sharing breakfast instead of two people bound together by necessity and a lie that's already taken root.

Patrick finishes his slice and wipes a crumb from his mouth with his thumb. He's watching me—steady, not intrusive, but not letting me dodge anything either.

"So," he says gently, "we need to talk through the plan for today."

Right. Today.

Town. Supplies. Stares. Whispers. And the funeral tasks I haven't touched yet.

"Aye," I say, pulling the notepad closer. "We've things that can't wait. Feed. Coffee. Lock for the lower shed. Staples for the east fence. And...I need tae stop by Magnolia & Moss." The words thicken. "Florist. For the service."

Patrick's posture shifts subtle, protective. Not pitying. Just...there. "What do you need from them?" he asks quietly.

"Roses. Thistles. Something simple." I force my pen to the paper. "Henry wrote it down in the will. No fuss. Just flowers and a hymn the pastor chooses."

His brows lift slightly—surprised, maybe, that I'm the one planning it. Or that I'm managing not to shake apart entirely.

"And calls," I add. "I've to ring Pastor Willis, the cemetery office, the funeral home. Fix the time. Confirm the order. Let folks know when they can come pay respects."

Patrick nods slowly. "We can handle that after town."

We.

I pretend that doesn't settle somewhere inconvenient in my chest.

He reaches for the ledger hanging by the pantry and tips his chin toward it. "Let's add what the place needs. Feed. Hardware. Whatever Henry was running low on."

"Ledger stays on the hook," I say automatically. "Always did."

He hands it to me instead of opening it, and I breathe through the pinch in my chest as I bring it to the table. I open to the last clean page and write a tidy column—scratch grain, mineral block, lock with heft, coffee before mine runs out.

Patrick adds gate staples, then glances toward the porch. "Birdseed too."

My throat tightens. "Aye. He'd complain if we forgot."

When the list is finished, I close the ledger and return it to its hook. Order where I can make it.

Patrick lingers at the table, fingers tapping lightly. "About the rest of it," he says. "Us."

I tense.

Not this again.

But he continues not pushing, just practical. "We already sorted most of our backstory. That's a good start, but the town gossips will look for proof today. We need to match what they expect to see."

I busy myself brushing crumbs off the table. "Ye mean smiles and foolishness."

"I mean consistency," he says. "So they don't question your claim on the land. Or Henry's wishes."

That stops me cold. My head snaps up. "What do ye know about Henry's wishes?"

He nudges his mug with one finger, calm as still water. "What you told me. When you said this place was meant for you. That he wanted you to have it."

I swallow hard. Did I say it out loud? Or did it leak out between words, soaked in grief, making my edges soft?

Either way, he heard me. Worse, he believed me.

"And," he adds gently, "if that's true, Mharie... then we have to play this smart. Together."

I look down at my bare hand. His gaze follows.

"No ring," I warn.

He doesn't flinch. "We'll circle back to it. Later. After we get through the day."

Later. Not now. I can live with later. We gather jackets and the list. Out the back door, the land greets us like an old dog rousing—sun warming the frost, cows shifting their weight, the air just crisp enough to pretend it's winter. Dougal watches us from the paddock with the expression of a delinquent teenager waiting for a chance to misbehave.

Patrick points at him. "Don't even think about it."

Dougal sneezes. *Make me.*

We take the truck into town with the windows cracked. Texas rolls out in long, low stretches—pasture and cedar and fences beaded with sparrows. In Scotland, the mountains press close, like they're holding you. Here the sky is a lidless eye. Both feel like home. Both feel like a loss.

Piper Falls wears Christmas the way the town always has—too much tinsel, too many lights, wreaths hung at slightly crooked angles that no one corrects because they were hung with love. Twice as Nice has a book tree again. I pretend it doesn't charm me.

Our first stop is Lone Star Feed & Tack. The bell clangs overhead, and the smell hits: leather, molasses, dust, cold air from the back storage room.

"Henry's girl," Earl Whitaker says gently from behind the counter. "Sorry for your loss, sweetheart."

I manage a nod. "Thank ye."

Martha Whitaker bustles forward and enfolds my hand in both of hers. "We've been prayin' for you. Anything you need, you let us know."

Dale pipes up from the end of the counter. "And this must be the fiancé."

"Patrick Williams," Patrick says, with a warm handshake and steady eyes.

Martha leans against the register, grinning like she already knows every detail we haven't even invented yet. "Lord above, you two are cute. No ring yet?"

I breathe once before answering. "We've been a bit distracted."

Her grin blooms. Of course it does. We take a cart and make our way down the aisles, loading what the homestead needs. Locks. Staples. Grain. Mineral block. Salt. A bag of birdseed I grab too quickly. At the counter, Martha tucks a packet of peanut brittle into our pile. "On the house. You look like you could use a little sweetness."

Two older women drift in, pretend to examine boots, and not-so-subtly examine us. One raises her phone. I raise a brow. She lowers it, flustered, then smiles.

She beams, all sweet intent. "We're just thrilled, dear. Whole town's been hoping somebody would step in and keep that place going."

A line inside me tightens not anger, just truth pressing up from the ache.

"Someone did," I say. "Me."

Her smile falters, then warms. "Of course. Yes, of course."

Patrick's hand presses lightly at the small of my back.

Not claiming.

Steadying.

I like it more than I want to.

We haul the bags of grain to the back of the truck. Patrick checks their balance twice—once like a rancher, once like a man who can't stop himself from making sure I don't strain my back. I pretend not to notice either.

"We've one more stop," I say as I climb into the passenger seat. "Magnolia & Moss."

Patrick nods, no hesitation, no question. "Lead the way."

Piper Falls is busy for midmorning. Cars line Main Street. Folks head into the bakery, the library, the diner. Above it all, the wreaths along the lampposts sway like they're nodding to us. We park outside Magnolia & Moss white brick, windows sprayed with faux snow, a wooden sign painted with green vines curling around the lettering. I've walked past it a thousand times but never needed to walk in like this. The bell sounds as we enter, delicate as windchimes.

Inside, the air is cool and fresh eucalyptus, pine, roses. Bouquets wait in metal buckets. A Christmas display sits in the corner, all red berries and white lilies and soft candle glow.

Caroline Marsh, owner, florist, gossip collector, peeks out from behind a wall of holly. Her eyes soften the second she sees me.

"Oh, sweetheart." She presses a hand to her chest. "I heard about Henry. I'm so sorry."

I swallow the lump in my throat. "Thank you."

She steps closer, lowering her voice. "He was a good man. A quiet one, but good all the way through."

"Aye," I manage.

"And this must be..." She glances at Patrick, a smile warming. "The fella who stepped in. Town's been talkin'."

Patrick extends a hand, polite but not overdone. "Patrick Williams."

"Well, aren't you a pretty picture." She shakes his hand before turning back to me. "What can I do for you today, honey?"

"I need flowers," I say. "For the service."

Her expression shifts—not pitying, but careful. "Do you know what Henry wanted?"

"Aye. Something simple. No fuss. Thistles, roses. White or soft colors. He wrote it down."

"Oh, that sounds like him." Caroline gestures toward a counter lined with vases. "Let's build you somethin' that feels like Henry."

Patrick stays a respectful step behind, hands in his pockets, as Caroline gathers options.

"Thistles aren't common down here," she says, "but we've got blue eryngium that passes. And I have fresh-cut Texas roses this morning."

She lays stems on the counter—white roses, dusty blue eryngium, eucalyptus, small sprays of baby's breath.

I trace the edge of a rose with my fingertip, the softness of it at war with the tightness in my chest.

"This looks right," I whisper.

Caroline nods. "I can do a casket spray and two arrangements for the front. Pickup day before the service? Or I can deliver."

"Pickup's fine." My voice steadies on a shallow inhale. "Thank you."

She rings it up slowly, like giving me time to breathe.

"If you need anything else," she murmurs, sliding the order slip across the counter, "you come back. No one in this town will let a Sutton girl carry her grief alone."

Patrick's gaze flicks to me at the word *Sutton*, but he doesn't comment.

Out on the sidewalk, the December sun feels too bright. Too loud.

I fold the paper and tuck it into my coat pocket. "That's done."

Patrick studies me, neither pushing nor prying. Just *seeing*.

"You all right?" he asks quietly.

I want to lie. I want to say yes. But my chest still feels split open.

"I will be," I say.

He nods once—like he believes me, like he'll hold that belief steady until I can do it myself.

We walk back to the truck. People glance as we pass, some politely, some with not-so-subtle curiosity.

Patrick opens my door before I can reach for the handle.

I arch a brow. "You're not my valet."

"No," he says, a faint smile tugging at his mouth. "But you looked like you could use the moment."

The moment.

A breath.

A quiet time to stand inside before the storm of the day starts again.

I take it.

Then I climb in, and Patrick rounds the hood, the late-morning sun cutting across his shoulders as if the day is choosing sides.

When he's in the driver's seat, when the engine rumbles to life, when the florist shop glows behind us—I finally feel the chapter closing on something old.

And opening on something I don't yet have a name for.

"Ready for the rest?" he asks.

"No," I admit. "But let's go anyway."

He smiles—small, steady—and pulls us into the road. The town watches.

The lie holds.

And something between us shifts, quiet as the first note in a song.

Chapter Nine

Patrick

The florist shop disappears in the mirror as we ease back onto Main Street, sunlight flashing off the Christmas tinsel strung between the lampposts. Mharie sits stiff in the passenger seat, one hand pressed over the folded flower order in her coat pocket. Her braid lies over her shoulder—neat, steady, far more composed than the thoughts clearly unraveling behind her eyes.

I don't push her to talk.

Sometimes grief sits like a weight on your chest. You just have to carry it until it shifts. I can't carry this for her, so I do the only thing I can: I drive the truck in silence until the storefronts fade and the road stretches wide ahead of us. Only then do I risk a glance at her. She's watching the horizon with that fierce, fractured determination she wears like armor.

"You all right?" I ask quietly, though the answer is already written across her face.

"No." Her voice isn't fragile—just honest. "I am so far from okay, but I'm going to do it anyway."

I nod once and keep driving. I believe her. She always does what she says she will. Past the town limits, the road opens into pale pasture, frost glittering like spilled salt. The sky is a wide, lidless eye overhead—making a person feel equally small and seen. She sits straighter the farther we go, hands folding and unfolding in her lap. Not healed. Not even close.

But clear with purpose. She finally breaks the silence. "Ye checked the east fence. What did ye actually see?"

I ease the truck onto the shoulder beside a stand of cedar. The engine ticks as it cools. The air between us shifts, expectation, worry, something else I can't quite name yet. I turn toward her fully.

"Three staples," I say. "All pried out clean. Someone used a claw hammer or fencing pliers. It wasn't Dougal."

Her breath stutters. "Not an accident, then."

"No." I lean forward, elbows on my knees. "Someone wants that fence to look weak. Wants the place to look neglected."

Her jaw locks. "Wendell."

"Maybe." I choose my words carefully. "I'm not pinning it on him yet. But whoever it was knew exactly what they were doing."

She presses her fingers to her forehead, fighting a wave of tangled fear, anger, and grief. "Henry took pride in this place. He'd be furious."

"And that's exactly why someone would target it," I say quietly.

She closes her eyes, lashes trembling. I let her sit with it—let her decide how to shoulder the truth. "What do we do?" she asks at last, voice tight.

"We document everything," I say. "Fix what we can. Keep track of every loose board and pried staple. And we stay three steps ahead until the funeral. After that? You and the lawyer can shut down any claim he tries."

She swallows hard. "And in the meantime? What do we do while we're trying to lay him properly to rest? He deserves peace."

"In the meantime," I say gently, "we make sure no one thinks this ranch is slipping."

Her gaze flicks to her bare left hand. Not because of me. Because she understands how a town works. How gossip becomes narrative. How narrative becomes leverage. If you don't control the story, it controls you.

"Patrick?" she asks, a hitch in her voice I'm not used to hearing.

"Yeah?" I brace for whatever comes next.

"For the ring... when we do talk about it proper... I don't want something fancy." Her voice barely edges above the hum of the heater. "Just something small. Silver. A pale stone. Something that doesn't shout our lie from a mile away. Something that says what it means without being overbearing."

I nod once, steady. "I'm not picking the ring, Mharie. You are."

Her lips part, surprised, as if she didn't realize she needed that choice.

"Oh," she whispers.

"Yeah," I say softly. "Oh. We can stop by a few places in town this week. If nothing feels right, we can drive up to Austin before the funeral."

She doesn't answer and I don't push. Not yet. I shift the truck back into drive. By the time the homestead comes into view, the sun is brushing gold across the barn roof. A faint ribbon of smoke curls from the chimney—embers banked low before we left, nothing burning unattended. Just enough to coax back to life.

December in Texas may pretend to be warm during the day, but the cold always comes back with the shadows.

We unload the truck in silence, grain in the feed room, coffee and flour on the porch bench. She moves on instinct: quick, competent, refusing to let grief slow her. But when I lift the last bag, she touches my arm to stop me. I set the bag back on the tailgate and turn to her.

"Tell me exactly what ye saw," she says again, steadier now, eyes sharp.

So I do. Every staple. Every scrape. Every mark that shouldn't have been there. She listens to all of it, jaw tight, eyes bright with anger and something deeper beneath it. When I finish, she nods once—resolute.

"We'll fix it," she says. Anything less is unacceptable.

"We will." The land deserves protecting. And so does she.

"And keep records."

"Every day."

"And no one touches the lower pasture locks except us."

"Agreed."

She exhales, long, shaky, but sure. "Aye."

For a moment, we stand together in the cool breath of winter, the cattle moving slow in the fading light, Henry's legacy pressing close. Then she squares her shoulders and climbs the porch steps.

"Thank you," she says without looking back.

Not for the fence. For not making her carry all of this alone. Inside, I coax the embers into a real fire and shovel a log beside it. She hangs her coat next to mine and moves straight to the table where the florist order lies, creased from her hands. She smooths it flat, tracing the stems she chose—thistle, rose, eucalyptus.

"It'll be a good service," I say quietly.

She nods, throat tight. "Aye. Henry would want something simple. No fuss. Just…honesty."

"It'll be that," I promise.

She blinks fast and turns toward the kettle. "Tea?"

"Yeah."

She fills it, the soft clink of metal settling into the quiet. Her movements are slower now, deliberate, measured, a woman holding herself together with routine. As she turns, her sleeve brushes Henry's old recipe box on the counter. It wobbles. She reaches to steady it and the lid shifts.

An envelope peeks out. Her name is written on the front. Not posted. Not sealed.

Just waiting.

Her breath stutters.

She hesitates—one second, two—then draws it free and sinks into the chair beside me. The paper is thick, slightly yellowed, like he'd been saving it for something important. His handwriting fills the page, neat, careful, a little shaky on the downstrokes.

Kid,

Didn't want to say all this over the phone. You've got a good head on your shoulders and more grit than most folks twice your age. I'm proud of you. Always have been. Wherever you go, whatever you do, just know you've still got a home here. This place will be yours someday—don't let anyone make you doubt that.

More when I see you at Christmas—

It ends there. Mid-thought. Mid-sentence. Mid-promise. Her fingers curl gently around the paper, careful not to crease it. A breath wavers out of her quiet, aching, held together by sheer will. She folds it along the original crease and tucks it into her coat pocket, close to her heart. When she turns, I'm already watching her, still and careful, knowing the wrong word could break her right open.

"You okay?" I ask softly.

"No." Then steadier: "But I will be. Henry may not have been my blood, but he was my family in every way that matters, and I will not let him down."

She shoves back from the table abruptly, gathers the mugs, and sits beside me. She doesn't drink right away. "I don't want tae pretend all the time," she murmurs.

"We won't," I say. "Only when we must."

Her gaze lifts sharp, searching. "And you'll tell me if something else happens. If someone touches the land again. If I'm going to prove I can keep this place, I can't be blindsided."

"Always."

She nods once, her hands curling around the mug like it anchors her. "Good." The fire snaps. Wind brushes the window. Something in her expression shifts soft, raw, and dangerously honest.

"Patrick?" she says.

"Yeah?"

"You don't have tae stay." Her voice is quiet. "But I'm glad you are."

That hits deeper than she knows.

"Me too," I say.

And it's the truest thing I've said all day.

Chapter Ten

Mharie

I'm awake before the sun has fully cleared the tree line. I head downstairs wrapped in Henry's old coat, with a restlessness that refuses to leave me be. It's no shock that Patrick is already in the living room, his voice low and even as he talks on the phone about delivery times and fittings, a cup of coffee at his side and a pencil in his hand. His calm works on my nerves like sandpaper. I don't remember the last time I felt relaxed.

So I slip out the back door.

The winter bite hasn't burned off yet. Texas mornings do that—cold enough to chafe your lungs, warm enough by lunch to make you doubt it ever happened. Frost clings to the grass in brittle lace. The homestead feels both familiar and foreign, like I've stepped into a version of my life I'm not fully wearing yet.

I head straight for the lower shed. Start where you can make a dent. The latch hangs crooked, twisted, as if someone had leaned on it with a pry bar. I oiled it last week. It slid smoothly then—neat, reliable, Henry-kept.

"Mo thruaighe," I whisper, and the metal is cold under my thumb as I trace the bend.

It isn't just the latch. The chain on the west trough has been swapped bright steel, cheap, too light. On the east fence line, a gate staple is missing. Not fallen. Not eased loose by the weather.

Gone.

Lifted clean.

My stomach tightens. There are innocent explanations. There always are. Wind. Wear. A neighbor is grabbing something in a hurry. But my skin prickles anyway.

Someone wants this place to look like it's slipping. "Ye sneaky gobshite," I mutter, though I don't say the name forming in the back of my teeth. "Whoever ye are."

A low mrrrph answers from behind me.

Dougal.

The ginger menace is chewing the corner of the hay tarp like he's doing the Lord's work. When he sees me, he rips a strip free, proud as you please.

"Mo chreach," I groan. "That's Henry's good tarp you *idjit.* You've got plenty of hay left in the rack!" I climb the fence with

a coil of rope and a temper needing a target. He chews faster. I shove my sleeves up in preparation. "Alright, lad. Playtime's over." Chaos is the only word to describe what follows, water buckets are overturned, cold water seeps into my boots, hens shout in offense, pigs bewildered, and me threatening stew in three languages. By the time I get him off the tarp and back in the paddock, the gatepost wobbles just enough to confirm a fresh problem.

Another weakness. Another place someone's been testing. I breathe long and slow, steadying myself. "Ye'll not take this from me," I murmur into the cold. "Not the land, not the peace of it. Not even an acre."

I head back to the barn looking for a distraction in morning chores. Chores help. I check troughs. Break the ice. Top water. The rhythm helps, but the small sabotages stack in the back of my mind like stones in a river. Two feed sacks have their seams picked, thread pulled loose in a way only deliberate hands manage.

"Coward," I say to the quiet. "Ye're a coward."

The quiet gives nothing back. When I turn, Dougal has the rope in his mouth, dragging it like a prize. He tosses his head. The rope slithers across the dirt.

"Drop it."

He does not. Two steps closer, he dances away. Two more, and he plants his hooves with smug determination. *"Chan eil,"* I scold, advancing with intent.

He relents. Dramatically. "I swear you do this on purpose," I mutter.

Then it's time for Nessa. She needs a stall ready before her transport arrives tomorrow. She deserves a warm, safe space. Or maybe I just need a win badly enough to chase one.

"Come on then, lass," I coax, bucket shaking. She flicks an ear. Judges me. Steps in the opposite direction with all the grace and none of the cooperation.

It becomes a dance, me circling low and steady, her drifting wide and disdainful, Dougal offering commentary from the fence like an underqualified supervisor. My bucket is no longer persuasion. It is an insult.

"All right. We'll make this easy."

Note: in fact, it is not easy.

Nessa sidesteps my advances like she's floating. She backs up like she's auditioning for the ballet.

Then—

"Mharie."

Patrick's voice rises behind me, close enough to lift the hairs along my arms. He stands at the paddock edge, sleeves rolled, sun catching the damp at his temples. The phone is gone. In his hand is a red apple.

Of course.

"She's not going to follow a bucket," he says mildly. "She'll follow a little sweetness though."

"Sweetness won't fix her," I retort. "Nessa is Dougal's daughter. She's four acres of stubborn wrapped in horns and a cute face. "

"May I?" His mouth twitches.

"I am not above watching you fail." He does not fail, and it only makes me want to kick the shite out of him more.

Coming into the paddock Patrick holds the apple out, lets her take a slow bite, steps back, and offers the rest. She follows as if it were her idea. In moments, he has her in the stall with the ease of a man born to it. He shuts the door with a clean click.

"Problem solved."

"I hate you."

"You don't."

"Numpty."

His smile edges into smug. "Thought you were about to swear yourself hoarse."

"It may not have been the best plan, but it was a plan," I grumble.

He steps closer. Not crowding. Not claiming. Just steady. "Everything alright?"

"No." The word slips out before I can reel it back. "The latch. The chain. The staple. Someone is trying to tear down what Henry built, and I cannae stand for it."

Patrick's jaw tightens fury on my behalf. "Then we act. We don't wait. We don't give whoever it is another inch on this land." He says it like fact. Like promise.

"What do we actually do?" My voice is low, tight. "Because I can't fight shadows, Patrick."

"Trail cams," he says without hesitation. "Motion lights. New hardware. And someone here keeping watch."

"Ye'll sit out here all night?" I lift a brow.

"If that's what it takes," he says simply. "I'll be on the porch. Just me and the dog. Anyone watching will know you're not alone."

The honesty of it hits harder than the words.

I snort softly. "We don't even have a dog."

He gives a crooked almost-smile. "Then I'll glare at the dark. Should work just as well."

A startled laugh escapes me. "Ye glare like a church elder who's found beer in the youth fridge."

"Effective, then," he says, deadpan.

Dougal noses toward the chicken coop like he's weighing his next bad idea. I level a look at him so sharp he rethinks his life choices. Patrick double-checks the stall latch, his hands sure, methodical, grounding.

When he straightens, he looks at me not pushing, not prying. Seeing me. "You don't have to do this all alone, Mharie."

Something tightens in my throat. "Maybe. But I don't know...where to start."

He nods toward the house. "Start with what we talked about yesterday."

My pulse skips. The ring. He doesn't say it, not out loud, but the meaning lands with weight and steadiness.

"You up for going into town?" he asks gently. "We can take our time. Walk through a few places. See what feels right."

I swallow hard, fingers curling around Henry's coat. "No," I whisper. "I am not up for it."

He nods once, accepting that without flinching. "Will you go anyway?" he asks.

I lift my chin. "Aye," I say. "Let's go."

His smile is small, warm, steady. "Then we'll go."

And for the first time since Henry died, the next step feels, just barely, like something I can take.

Chapter Eleven

Patrick

My phone buzzes. Adam. "Why isn't Nessa already here?" he demands without a hello. "And why is Hank driving south to pick her up?"

"Hello to you too, Brother. So good to hear from you. I'm fine, how are you?" I drop the sarcasm and answer his question. "Some things came up. I'll be here awhile."

"What kind of things? Do I need to fly down?"

"No." Too sharp. I soften it. "No, I've got it handled."

"Pat—"

"I said I've got it. Trust me." Silence stretches. Adam doesn't like being shut out. Finally, he exhales.

"Fine. But you'd better have a damn good reason."

"I do," I say—and hang up before he can press further.

Through the window, I spot Mharie crossing the yard toward the feed room, shoulders squared against the morning chill. She moves briskly, purposeful, like a woman who refuses to be slowed by grief. Dougal trails behind her several paces, pretending he's not following her but absolutely following her.

I shrug on my jacket and step outside. Mharie is bent over the feed-room latch when I reach her brow furrowed, jaw locked hard enough to crack a tooth.

"This was fine yesterday," she mutters, tracing the bent metal. "Now it's twisted like someone leaned their whole weight on it with something sharp."

I crouch beside her and trace the fresh scrape marks. Sharp. Clean. Not weather. Not animal. "Not subtle, are they?" I say quietly. "They tried to make it look like Dougal did this but no horns on the planet would cause marks like this."

She shoots me a sharp look—not at me, but at the truth of it. "They're getting bold. They want me rattled."

"They're trying to make the place look neglected," I confirm. "Fence staples. Latches. Chains. Now this."

Her throat works. She's angry, but beneath that—worn thin.

"Whoever's doing it," she says, voice low, "they think I'm too distracted to notice."

I shake my head. "They're wrong."

She exhales once tight, controlled but her fingers curl into a fist on top of the latch.

"Patrick," she says softly, "this isnae just sabotage. This is sending a message."

"I know," I answer. "And we'll send one back."

Before we get back in the house, Dougal noses the feed-room door again—just enough to test it, to see if it'll give. When he notices me watching, he freezes...then slowly—*very slowly*—turns and strolls away like he had simply been admiring the hinges. I narrow my eyes. He pretends he doesn't see.

Mharie exhales and rubs her forehead. "I dinnae know where to start today. Every time I fix one thing, something else looks wrong."

"That's why you don't do it alone."

Her gaze lifts sharply, defensive out of habit, and I can't bring myself to be offended; instead, I gesture toward the truck. "Let me take you to dinner."

Her head snaps up. "Dinner?"

"Yeah. Not barbecue in a paper tray or a burger in a wrapper. Let me take you somewhere with real napkins, a waiter, and a view. You've been here for how long and haven't left except to buy locks and birdseed. I was looking online and found a place down by the falls. We can have dinner and talk about the homestead."

Her mouth quirks not quite a smile but close enough, I'll take it. "And to talk about a ring," she says quietly, not looking at me.

"Talk," I echo. "Look. If we find something that fits, then we buy."

Her shoulders stiffen like she's bracing for impact.

"Think of it as a promise," I say gently. "Not ownership. Not pressure. Just me telling every nosy bastard in town—and you—that I'm all in on helping you keep this place."

She lifts her chin. "And what does the ring say to *me*?"

"That you're not alone," I answer. "That I'm here. That I'm staying. And if you don't like any part of it, we walk out without one. No questions asked."

She studies me, searching for the catch, the push, the lie, but there isn't one. At this time, in this moment, on this day, I only want to be here for this woman who is quickly becoming more important to me than I want to examine too closely.

Her jaw works once, twice, before she exhales, a small surrender wrapped in steel. "One dinner," she mutters. "And...aye. We'll go. We'll look and maybe we will buy." The wind lifts her braid as it whips around the barn. She studies my face like she's checking for loose screws.

"Somewhere quiet," she says finally, conceding like she's sacrificing a piece in chess. I'll take the win before she changes her mind.

"Aurora Heights. Rooftop. Steaks. Real napkins."

Her mouth curves. "Real napkins?"

"Real napkins and, if we're lucky, tiramisu."

"Let's hope then," she turns toward the house and I follow behind her.

The bell over the door of Twice as Nice jingles when we step inside. The shop smells faintly of cedar and lemon polish. Mrs. Jenkins straightens immediately, eyes dropping—instinctive-ly—to Mharie's bare left hand.

"Good evening, you two! How can I help you? Looking for something special?"

"Something simple," Mharie manages.

I stay a half-step behind her. Mrs. Jenkins brings out a tray gold, rose gold, silver. Stones that shout in reds and blues. Stones that whisper in sparkling white and pale yellows. Mharie stands there, fingers trailing over the offerings until she gets to the final ring. Soft. Pale. Winter-clear. Silver band, clean and unfussy. A moonstone. Mharie touches it lightly as if she's afraid it'll vanish if she lets it go.

"You like that one?" I ask.

She swallows but I see the answer in her eyes before she finds her words. "I...aye. I do."

"Then it's yours." I nod at Ms. Jenkins who smiles and moves to grab a ring box and to process the sale. While I give her my credit card, Mharie tries it on, and I swear, in that moment, time stops. The stone glows—soft, opalescent, shifting with the light nestled against her pale skin as if it was made for her.

"It doesn't shout," she murmurs.

"It tells the truth," I counter. "You're steady. You're here. And you're not alone."

Her eyes flick up to mine, just once but it's enough.

Mrs. Jenkins wraps the ring box even though the ring already sits on Mharie's hand. She wishes us both a good night as we walk out the door. Once outside, Mharie looks down at the moonstone glowing softly on her finger. Her thumb grazes it, slow and thoughtful, like she's still testing whether it feels like belonging.

No flourish.

Just acceptance quiet, deliberate, and entirely hers.

We swing by the feed store before dinner. The clerk recognizes her immediately and offers condolences that make her shoulders stiffen. I sign for the fittings, the new chain, and the gravel bags she requested. The clerk loads the truck bed.

"You two take care now," he says, glancing meaningfully at the ring.

Mharie exhales through her nose. Hard. "I swear," she mutters as we get back in the truck, "I am one 'congratulations' away from biting someone."

"That will have the biddies gossiping for sure." Mharie snorts, and I can't help but chuckle. We drive with windows cracked and the radio low. Christmas lights glow across town, some perfectly straight, others leaning like they had too much eggnog. Piper Falls hums—firefighters grabbing coffee, the librarian duking it out with a stubborn wreath, and half the town pretending not to stare as we drive by.

"It's strange," she murmurs. "Being noticed but no' seen."

"It'll level out."

"Does anything level out in a town like this?"

"Sometimes you trade the questions for casserole."

Half a smile. Aurora Heights gleams above the river. The host clocks the ring but only smiles and seats us by the railing. She orders salmon. I order steak.

"I talked to Adam," I say.

"What did ye tell him?"

"That Hank's handling Nessa. And I'm staying here. He offered to fly down. I said no."

"Because?"

"Because I don't want him here. Not yet."

Relief flickers across her face quick, guilty.

"He'd mean well."

"He always means well. But he's not subtle, he's a bulldozer, and this needs subtle."

"Aye. It does."

We eat. Quiet. Peaceful.

"You ever think about staying?" I ask.

"Here?"

"Yeah."

She laughs softly. "I think about leaving every time I step onto the porch. I think about staying every time the wind moves through the grass." She stares at the falls but sees something else. "Back home, in Glencoe, I fought for that internship like a scrapper. Poured tea for men who thought I was the help. It felt like purpose, a means to an end, a life I had always wanted. Here feels like roots, like history and destiny and a future me that is not quite realized. I want both and it kills me that I can't have them."

"You can have both for a while," I say gently. "Or build something new that looks nothing like you planned but everything like what's possible." She lifts her cup. The ring glows.

A woman at another table leans over. "Sorry for your loss. And congratulations."

"Thank you," Mharie says steadily.

When they leave, she exhales. "That one I can take."

"If anyone tries a speech," I say, "I'll pretend to choke."

"Do, and I'll let ye."

Coffee cools slowly in our cups. Tiramisu disappears one forkful at a time. The world beyond the railing fades into darkness, broken only by the falls' shimmer. Night deepens—and with it, something between us. Not loud. Not bold. Just steady, like a truth settling into place. She's quiet, thoughtful, fingers brushing the silver band now and then as if testing its weight.

She toys with the ring without thinking, and when she notices, she stops herself.

"You meant the promise?" she asks.

"All of it."

"What does all of it look like for you?"

"A thousand little things. Fixing posts. Ordering fittings. Keeping watch. Staying until you don't need me—and maybe a bit longer."

She nods. Slowly. Like we've struck an unspoken bargain.

The drive back is quiet. Easy. At the homestead, the porch light glows warm. Dougal snorts. Nessa shifts in her stall.

"Thank you," she says softly.

"For dinner?"

"For... not letting them write a story I don't want."

"I promised."

She hesitates at the doorway, fingers brushing the wood like she's steadying herself. "Will you sit out awhile?"

"Yeah," I say. "I'll keep watch."

She nods small, tired, honest and slips inside. The porch light casts a warm square onto the steps, softening the edges of the night.

I settle into the porch chair facing the yard, boots planted, breath visible in the cool air. Tomorrow will be long: the service at half-past ten, the graveside after, the line of people who loved Henry and the ones who only loved a good story. She'll have to carry more than any one person should.

So tonight? Tonight isn't about fences or trail cams. Tonight is about giving her a little peace before the weight of tomorrow arrives. A coyote yips somewhere past the far fence. I stand until the sound fades back into the dark, then sit again, steady and still. I don't know if anyone's watching the homestead. But I know she's watching me keep my word.

So I stay.

Not guarding the land. Guarding the quiet she needs before morning comes.

Chapter Twelve

Mharie

I don't want to be here.

Mick Reynolds's office isn't a place anyone visits on a good day, but today it feels tiny like the walls are pressing in on me. He shuts the door gently, as though the room itself might shatter if handled wrong.

"We'll keep this short," he says, settling behind his desk.

"First hearing's set for December twenty-ninth. Preliminary only judge wants to review the filings and decide if Wendell has standing." Twenty-ninth. Four days after Christmas. The idea of sitting in a courtroom while garlands come down feels like a punch to the ribs.

"What does he even have to stand on?" I ask, my fingers tightening around the folder Mick slides toward me.

"Bloodline," he says simply. "That's his angle. You were chosen, not born. Some judges give weight to that."

Heat crawls up my face, and I can feel it coloring my cheeks. "Blood is the least important thing, and I know that because Henry taught me."

"I know," Mick says gently. "But the court wants proof you're running the homestead. Feed bills, grain orders, vet notes, repairs everything. Keep it organized. Show consistency."

"Competence," I echo, though it tastes bitter. "Aye. I understand."

Patrick sits beside me, steady and infuriatingly calm. "And if Wendell's interfering?"

Mick shakes his head. "Without proof, it's just suspicion. Judges won't touch it."

I swallow hard. Proof. As if the bent latch and swapped chains haven't screamed enough.

Mick stands. "I'm sorry today is what it is. Henry was a good man."

"He was," I whisper and it nearly breaks me.

We step outside into a day that feels too bright for mourning, and before I know it, we're walking toward the church. When we get there, it's packed.

Too packed.

Flowers along every pew. Slow hymns hum beneath the low murmur of familiar voices. Women from town smoothing foil over casseroles on the back table Texans grieve by cooking enough to feed an army. My pulse stumbles when I see Jake near the back. Not a kid anymore, but still so young, holding his hat like he doesn't know what to do with his hands. His eyes are rimmed red. Henry loved him. And Jake... he'd loved Henry too. He gives me a tiny nod. I return it, throat tight.

Patrick follows me to the front pew; the one reserved for family. He doesn't touch, doesn't press he just sits close enough that the warmth of him anchors me to the bench. I grab a tissue from one of the boxes that liberally dot the pew. The pastor speaks. His voice carries through the rafters steady, warm, the kind of voice that's buried more ranchers than he can count. People stand and take turns sharing memories one by one: stories of fences fixed in the rain while cursing the mud, calves delivered at three a.m. with nothing more than baling twine and stubbornness. Neighbors speak about how he'd show up before dawn with a thermos of black coffee for anyone working a hard shift, then join them.

Every story tells the tale of a man who made his life a legacy of compassion and love and who carved his place in a town that would never forget him.

When we walk to the cemetery, the winter air cuts sharper than it did an hour ago. The grass crunches under our boots, frost clinging to every blade. Someone's breath hitches behind me. Someone else sniffles. The sky is swollen and gray, like it's holding back for our sake, and even then it is a mercy. The pastor's voice softens as he begins the final prayer. The wind shifts, carrying the faint scent of pine from the tree line. When the first handful of dirt hits the casket, the sound is a dull, hollow thump final in a way I wasn't ready for. The second thump cracks something inside me. The third nearly brings me to my knees.

Patrick's hand finds the small of my back, solid and warm, just enough to steady, not enough to hold. A quiet offering of strength in a place where everything else inside me is breaking.

My voice cracks on the whisper. "Goodbye, Papa Henry."

With those words my world fractures in a way I didn't think was possible anymore, leaving everything slightly off-center from what it was an hour ago. As the ceremony ends, we slip away before someone can catch my arm, before another memory can be pressed into my hands like a weight I can't carry. Outside the gate, the cold air bites, sharp enough to anchor me but not enough to steady me. Patrick drifts two steps closer, guiding us across the square toward the truck without saying a word.

Where Wendell is waiting.

Of course he is.

Leaning on his dented Silverado like it grants him authority, hat tipped low, smirk carved into place as if he practiced it in the mirror.

"Well," he drawls. "Sad day."

"Not sad enough to keep you away," I snap.

He tsks. "Just paying respects. Though I hear you had a meeting this morning." His gaze slides to the moonstone ring on my finger. "Convenient timing."

Patrick bristles next to me. "Wendell, don't start running your mouth about shit you don't know."

Wendell's grin sharpens.

"*You* don't get to scold me, city boy. You barely know which end of a ranch is up."

Patrick doesn't blink. "Still own more ranch, thank you."

Wendell scoffs, his eyes flicking to me, cold and cutting, before he climbs into his truck and peels away like the road owes him deference.

My hands shake with fury. With grief. With everything.

"You alright?" Patrick asks softly.

"No," I rasp. "But walking away was the only thing stopping me from hitting him with something heavy."

"Mick would advise against that."

"I dinnae care what Mick advises."

A faint breath of amusement slips out of him not quite a laugh, just the ghost of one.

"Come on. Let's get you home."

We climb into the truck in silence.

Halfway down the county road, Patrick huffs... then outright laughs under his breath.

I turn, incredulous. "What's so funny?"

It's been a day of grief and grit and sharp edges there's no humor in any of it for me.

He shakes his head, still grinning. "Wendell told me I didn't know which end of a ranch is up. Keeps calling me 'city boy.'"

I blink. "Aye. He did."

Patrick's grin widens, dry and disbelieving.

"I don't think he realizes I own more land than he could dream of."

Despite everything the funeral, the fight, the ache still pounding beneath my ribs a startled, unwilling snort escapes me.

"Eejit," I mutter. "Both of you."

But the tightness in my chest eases, just a fraction.

Enough to breathe.

The house smells like flowers and casseroles lasagna, chicken spaghetti, banana bread. Enough to feed the whole county. Texans mourn loudly and practically. I thank the last pair of women who step inside, but the words crumble in my mouth. They squeeze my hand, leave me to the quiet.

I can't be still.

I change out of my dress immediately, the black fabric landing in a heap on the bedroom floor. Boots. Jeans. Flannel. Clothes I can breathe in.

Then I walk straight outside.

No words.

No explanations.

Just work.

The cold bites at my sleeves as I check troughs, stack feed, straighten boards that don't want to straighten. My muscles burn. My breath fogs in the air. Grief settles into my bones like frost.

Patrick eventually falls into step beside me. Silent. Matching my pace. Fixing a loose board. Checking a gate hinge. Not asking anything he knows I can't answer right now.

"The funeral was hard," he says finally. Simple. Not prying.

I nod once.

"You don't have to prove the right to stand here," he says quietly. "Not today."

"Aye." My voice is thin but steady. "Not to you. Never to you."

He nods once, accepting that without prying. We work until my breathing evens out and the weight in my chest settles. The winter air bites, the light still bright and high, nowhere near evening. But grief makes time strange. Every minute feels like an hour.

When I finish tying off the last line, my arms ache and my palms sting. Patrick watches me set the rope aside, then steps close enough that his shoulder almost brushes mine.

"You ready to go in for a bit?" he asks.

I don't trust my voice, so I nod. Inside, the house greets us with quiet dishes on the counter, flowers by the sink, the soft hum of a refrigerator that suddenly feels too loud in the stillness. I walk through it all, past the casseroles and condolences, needing space more than anything.

In Henry's room, the air holds traces of cedar oil and old paper, the familiar scent grounding me the moment I step in. I don't lie down on the bed. I don't collapse into a pile on the floor. I sit on the edge of the bed, hands folded tight in my lap, letting the quiet settle around me.

Grief crests in a slow, heavy wave that threatens to take me under; beneath it, something fiercer rises. Something that feels like a resolve. The whisper comes out rough but unwavering.

"Cha toir mi seachad seo."

I will not give it up.

Not the land. Not Henry's legacy. Not my place here.

Let Wendell try. Let the hearing come.

I'm not done. Not beaten. Not backing down.

Chapter Thirteen

Patrick

Hank rattles up the drive just after two p.m., his trailer clattering like it's held together by stubbornness and bailing wire; only a man who's hauled stock his whole life would trust it. Hank kills the engine, climbs out, and immediately grumbles like he's been rehearsing it.

"Dammit, Pat," he calls, slapping the dust off his jeans. "Why am *I* the one doing this run? I swear, if one more person bails on me last second "

"You said you were coming through anyway," I remind him.

"Coming through, not playing delivery boy." He squints at me. "Adam owes me for this."

"He said you owed me," I counter.

Hank snorts. "Well, one of you liars needs to get your stories straight."

The screen door creaks behind us. Mharie steps out onto the porch, still in the work clothes she changed into the moment we got home from the funeral. Her hair is tugged loose from its braid, her face pale from crying she'd never admit to, her expression carved down to something flat and steady. She walks toward the paddock without a word, hands shoved into Henry's old coat, jaw set like stone. By the time she reaches the fence, she's braced against it white-knuckled grip on the rail, breathing slow and controlled like she's forcing herself to stay upright.

She hasn't said much since we left the cemetery. I haven't pushed. Nessa snorts, ears flicking toward the rattle of Hank's grain bucket.

"Alright, sweetheart," Hank calls to her, shaking the bucket like he's coaxing a queen. "Let's make this easy."

For a moment, Nessa plants her feet and sizes him up like she's deciding if she's in a mood. Dougal watches nearby with the enthusiasm of a man instigating a bar fight. But then Nessa steps forward, regal as ever, and walks into the trailer like she's inspecting high-class accommodations.

Hank beams. "See? She likes me."

"She likes food," Mharie says, voice flat but not sharp.

Hank chuckles and hands me the paperwork. We lean against the cold fender of his truck to sign. His brows lift as he watches my name go on the line.

"So," he says slowly, "you're staying out here awhile?"

"For now."

"That's new." His tone isn't judgment just observation with teeth. "Adam knows?"

"He does."

Hank studies me for a long beat, then folds the papers neatly. "Alright then. Just don't make me drive all the way back down here in a week because you came to your senses."

I roll my eyes. "Thanks for the vote of confidence."

He points at me, then at the house. "You owe me barbecue."

"Put it on my tab."

He climbs back into the cab, still muttering about being the town's unpaid labor force, and hauls out, trailer clattering behind him. When the dust settles, the homestead feels... emptier. Nessa wasn't loud, but she filled space.

A beat passes. Then another. Work breaks the silence first. "We should check the east post," I say.

"Aye," she answers, already turning toward it.

No hesitation. No pause. We walk the fence line, boots crunching frost-bitten grass. The wobbly post waits for us, leaning just a little. I dig out the base while she braces the post, her shoulder steady against the weight.

Our arms brush once. I feel it everywhere.

"Too far left," I say.

"It's straight."

"It's leaning."

"No' as much as you think."

Her braid slides over her shoulder as she shifts to hold the post. I swallow hard, doing my best to focus on the gravel and dirt and not the woman anchoring the post beside me. We tamp the ground tight in place until it holds solid.

"One thing done," she murmurs.

I nod. "More tomorrow."

She doesn't answer, but her jaw flexes. Determination. Grief sharpened into something usable.

We check the shed latch next to see fresh scrape marks. Dougal had been in pasture all day. There is no denying it, someone was here.

My spine tightens, but I don't say anything yet. Not until I've got proof. Mick made that clear.

"I'll reinforce this later," I say lightly.

"Aye."

Her voice is low. Controlled. Too controlled. We finish the outside work in silence and head toward the porch. She doesn't go inside. She detours to the feed shed, grabs a scoop, and starts the back pasture rounds like it's any other day. I don't say a word, just grab a bale of hay and follow. Not to hover. Just to be there to share the load.

By the time we move inside, the sun has shifted but hasn't even brushed evening yet. The house is warm from the casseroles lining the counters and whatever kindness-filled hands dropped them off after the funeral. She doesn't speak, just sets Henry's ledger on the table and flips it open. I make tea. She doesn't thank me. I don't expect her to. I sit across from her, elbows on the table, watching her rebuild structure in neat columns. Watching her fight to stay upright.

Her hand drifts once just once to the moonstone ring still on her finger. A glance, a breath, nothing more.

She doesn't acknowledge it.

Neither do I.

When she closes the ledger, her shoulders sag. Not defeated just exhausted.

"You done for now?" I ask.

"Aye."

We step onto the porch. The swing creaks under our weight, mugs cooling between our palms. Evening settles across the pasture. Dougal snorts from his pen, and the rest of the herd calls back. Mharie stares straight ahead, eyes distant but fierce.

After a long stretch of silence, she whispers, "It's never enough, is it?"

"What isn't?"

"The work. The proof. The fighting."

I reach out, barely brushing my fingers against her forearm. Not a hold. Not even contact, not really. Just presence.

"You don't have to prove anything to me."

She doesn't look at me, but she nods once. I'll take it. Today was rough for everyone but more so for her. We sit in silence until the cold eats through our coats. When she finally stands, it's slow, careful.

"I'm going to lie down," she murmurs.

"Alright."

The door clicks shut behind her, soft, final. The kind of sound that says she's held herself together as long as she can... and now she's allowed to stop.

I stay on the porch.

Cold air settles across the pasture in a slow, creeping hush. The fence line stands dark against the pale grass. The trail toward the road stays empty. Too empty. Those scrape marks on the shed weren't old. Someone's been testing the edges of this place, seeing what they can loosen before anyone notices. Unfortunately for them, we notice everything. I grab the box of cameras from the truck, tucking it under one arm as I cross the yard. My boots crunch through frost, loud in the heavy quiet. The ladder's cold metal stings my hands when I drag it into place.

One camera at the gatepost.

One by the barn.

One facing the shed where the hinge was scratched; next time we will know the score.

Each camera I click into place steadies something in me. A focus. A purpose. Something I can fix while she's carrying enough grief for both of us.

I test the angles twice, maybe three times. Maybe overkill. But overkill is still better than "we can't prove it," and Mick's voice is still stuck in my head. By the time the last camera locks into its bracket, the cold has crept through my jacket. My breath hangs in front of me in long, steady clouds. The kind of breath you draw when you're preparing for a long fight.

I scan the pasture one more time. Nothing moves except the wind through the dry grass.

Good.

Let it stay that way.

When I climb the porch steps again, a soft light spills from Henry's old bedroom window. I know she's in there trying to sleep, trying to breathe through grief that doesn't lift when the work is done and your mind wanders. I can't stop the grief. but I can keep her safe. I settle onto the porch swing, the wood cold beneath me, and let the chains creak their familiar rhythm.

I'll keep watch tonight. Not because she asked. Because she shouldn't have to ask. And because for the first time since setting foot in Piper Falls I know exactly where I'm meant to be.

Right here.

Guarding what she refuses to lose.

Chapter Fourteen

Mharie

Morning starts with the kettle and the back door banging against Patrick's hip. He comes in on a breath of cold, hay in his hair. His boots leave a tidy trail of frost on the mat. "South pen's fine," he says, shouldering the door closed. "North latch is thinking about being a poet."

"Melodramatic?" I ask, reaching for the tin of tea.

"Unreliable with timing."

"Ah." I hand him the little jar of oil from the junk drawer. "Give it a verse."

He pockets it with a grin and slides into our usual places. We've fallen into a rhythm that feels like a lullaby you learn by accident: mismatched mugs, two slices off last night's bread, his thumb finding the radio knob without looking. The house listens, pleased we remembered how.

We eat on our feet. He chooses the end slice, which I cut too thick; I take the heel that tastes like yesterday and cinnamon. He watches me lick butter off my thumb and pretends he isn't watching. I pretend I don't feel it. When he reaches around me to snag the jar of honey, the brush of his jacket sleeve at my shoulder makes my breath trip and then find itself again.

"Feed store today," I say, wiping crumbs into my palm. "Mineral, scratch grain, staples, birdseed."

"Birdseed," he echoes, as if the word itself is a promise.

The yard breathes white when we step outside. The morning's cold isn't mean, just insistent. We split off without deciding—my lane to the hens and Dougal; his to the shed, the trough, and those latches that have become characters in a saga he's determined to end. I scatter feed with my wrist loose the way Henry taught me, and the hens cluck approval. Dougal lowers his shaggy head and nudges my hip until I rub the spot between his horns that turns him into a calf again.

"Greedy boy," I murmur. He huffs, pleased.

By the time I meet Patrick at the north gate, he's knelt in the thin mud, shoulder braced, breath smoking. Oil gleams on the hinge like a small mercy.

"Try her," he says.

I swing. The latch catches clean and sure. "Saints be praised."

"Don't go making me a saint yet," he says, standing. "I'm still negotiating with the back trough."

"Tell it the union won't hold."

He laughs, the sound short and warm. When he reaches for the coil of wire at my feet, his shoulder nudges mine. Neither of us moves. The world tilts a fraction and rights itself.

"There's a spot on the south line where the cedar's rubbing," he says. "We'll need to trim it before it eats the wire."

"We?" I say.

"We," he answers, simple as a fence post.

He wipes his hands on a towel that used to be white, then glances sideways at me—just long enough to say he remembers the thing I said earlier, when I tried to make it sound casual.

"Still want to head down for the lighting?" he asks.

My stomach does a ridiculous little turn because I hadn't meant to suggest it like an invitation. I'd only muttered it while we were loading scratch grain—*Henry always took me, it's tradition*—and then pretended the chickens were suddenly fascinating.

But he remembered.

I find my cap and tug it low. "Might as well try to belong to the tradition again."

Lone Star Feed & Tack smells like molasses, leather, and the dust of ten thousand conversations nobody can remember starting. The bell over the door throws its shoulders back and shouts when we walk in.

Martha looks up from the counter, pencil behind her ear, a candy cane stuck at a jaunty angle in the corner of her mouth. "Well, if it isn't my favorite homestead duo," she sings. "Morning, sugar. How's your list?"

"Longer than it has any right to be," I say. "Mineral, scratch, staples, and birdseed."

Patrick tilts his head at the aisle. "I'll grab the blocks."

We move together down the feed row, cart wheels chattering over grooves a hundred years deep. It's three steps into familiar when the temperature in the room shifts at our backs. I feel it the way you do a cold front through a crack.

"Campbell," comes a voice that always sounds like it's leaning on something. "Williams."

Royce looks precisely like a man who's been waiting to say our names out loud: satisfied with himself, bored with the options.

Most folks in Piper Falls know him as Wendell Sutton's shad-ow—always nearby, always listening, the kind of man who mis-takes proximity for importance. He works odd jobs, knows every scrap of gossip before it hits the sidewalk, and carries himself like a self-appointed foreman of everyone else's business.

"Afternoon," I say, because I was raised right.

Martha snorts from behind the counter. "Don't feed him; he follows you home."

Royce smiles in a way that says he still believes small-town is a schedule he runs. "Hard to keep a place together this time of year. Fences go slack. Takes a steady hand. It would be a shame for a girl to get in over her head."

"I'm not," I place a bag of minerals in the cart, " in over my head."

"Mm." His gaze slides to Patrick, as if effort ought to be a men-only topic. "You co-signing that plan, Williams? Or are you just... passing through?"

Patrick doesn't rise. He doesn't widen his stance or fix his mouth into a line that says fight. He just sets the second mineral block in the cart and shifts until his sleeve grazes mine when I breathe.

Royce's eyes flick back to me—sharp, measuring. He's always been that way around Henry's place. Not cruel, just... oppor-tunistic. The kind of man who grew up watching the Suttons circle this land for decades and figured he'd get his chance to shine if he echoed the right opinions. To him, I'm the interruption. The outsider Henry chose on purpose. And men like Royce don't like choices they didn't make.

"Seems like she didn't ask me to co-sign anything," Patrick says, easy. "But since you're curious—the south fence is tight, and if you hear bawlin', it's probably you."

My laugh slips out without permission. Royce's smile thins.

"I know a few fellas could take those calves off your hands," he adds, and his tone says charity and his eyes say something else. "Before you're stuck with more than you can manage."

"I'll keep my calves," I say. "You keep your fellas."

He opens his mouth for another line he's been polishing. Before he can use it, Patrick touches my wrist. It isn't a show. It isn't a rescue. It's a question asked in skin: You all right?

I nod, because I am and I'm not, and both are true.

Then he bends, just enough, and kisses me.

His mouth is warm and unhurried, and the world blurs at the edges like we stepped out of bright into soft. I taste peppermint from Martha's candy canes and winter air. The heater ticks. Someone in the back drops a bucket. The bell over the door tings at nothing. None of it matters for three long heartbeats.

When he lifts his head, my pulse is doing somersaults. Royce looks like he bit a clove. Martha's grin could power the square.

"Well," she says, bright as a bell. "Engagement discount applies to minerals today."

Patrick blinks. "There's an engagement discount?"

"There is now," Martha says, triumphant. "Dale! Come help load this order before Royce runs us all over with that mouth of his."

Royce clears his throat and peels himself off the dog food. "Watch those calves," he says, but the edge is gone. He tips his cup like a hat at no one and leaves.

The breath I'd been holding goes out slowly.

On the way out, Martha slides a packet of peanut brittle across the counter. "For later," she says.

"Thank you."

We park on the side street near the church and join the flow—hats, scarves, mittens that don't match and don't need to. The big tree in front of the courthouse towers dark, ornaments like sleeping planets.

Patrick steers us toward the church booth where Mrs. Dunlap reigns. Her hair is perfect; her expression says she is in charge of cocoa and possibly, if pressed, the world.

"Two," Patrick says, handing over a five.

She eyes the money, then our linked hands, then my face the way women who love a town do—cataloging, approving, ready to scold if necessary. "Refills are free if you smile," she says, ringing a bell hung from her wrist. "And if you don't, I'll make you."

"I'm terrified," I tell her.

"You should be," she says, then softens. "Henry would be pleased to see you here."

"I hope so," I say, and the words shake a little.

We drift toward the tree, cocoa warming my fingers through ceramic. People do the thing towns do when they know they're in a story: talk louder, stand closer, pretend they're not watching you and absolutely are. There's a hum around us that isn't unfriendly—just thorough. That's Henry's girl. That's the Williams boy. They look right together. A little sting and a little balm.

The mayor clambers onto the temporary stage with a stack of index cards that looks like a small novel. He spreads his arms. The microphone squeals then forgives him.

"Friends, neighbors, and folks just passing through," he booms. "Welcome to the opening night of Piper Falls' Winter Carnival!"

Cheers rise like breath in cold air. The lights strung between buildings tremble.

"I had a few thoughts prepared on the meaning of community—"

"Plug it in, Larry!" someone yells, and the square laughs because it's already written this play.

"—which I will save for Sunday morning," he concedes, and the applause could tip the tree.

He glances at a volunteer by the switch. "Are we ready?" The volunteer gives a solemn thumbs-up only a seventeen-year-old can manage. "All right then! Ten... nine..."

The square becomes a single body counting down, breath bated.

"...three... two... one!"

Light erupts.

The tree blazes gold and green, a thousand tiny suns. Gasps rip through the crowd, and we all crane toward the storefronts as cords are tugged and the paper skins slip away up and down Main Street in a ragged, glorious reveal, behind the glass: whole worlds.

From here, I can't see details, and I don't try. That's for tomorrow tonight is about the gasp. The way the town makes a sound together and turns toward itself with pride.

Patrick's fingers thread into mine. Not for show, not because anyone's watching. Because the lights came on and he reached for me like that's what you do when the dark lifts.

"You look like you might stay," he says quietly, almost like he didn't mean to let it out.

"Maybe," I say, and the word feels braver than I do.

On the drive home, we don't talk much. When we pull into the drive, the porch light I left on throws a soft puddle onto the steps, and the ghost of Henry's boots on the mat steadies me instead of hollowing me out.

Patrick sets the mineral by the mudroom door. I put the birdseed inside the threshold so I'll trip over it in the morning and remember the feeder before anything else.

"Tomorrow," he says, voice pitched low, "we'll trim that cedar. And maybe go back to the square after chores—walk the windows, vote."

"Talk me into hot chocolate twice in two days?" I ask, pretending I need to talk about anything.

"I'll try my best."

At the kitchen doorway, we do an awkward dance we've perfected—goodnight in the hall where our rooms split.

"Goodnight, Mharie," he says.

"Goodnight, Patrick."

He hesitates, then lifts my hand and kisses the back of it, quick as a secret, like the feed store all over again, but this time just for the walls and the dark and me.

I stand there for a heartbeat after he's gone. Tomorrow there will be chores, town, and people. There will be calls from the solicitor I don't want, and a man in the next room whose laughter is starting to live in my mind.

Tonight there's the echo of a kiss that wasn't a performance, a square that made a sound like joy when the lights came on, and a maybe that didn't frighten me.

For now, that's enough.

Chapter Fifteen

Patrick

The whole of Piper Falls smells like gingerbread and cinnamon and maybe just a little too chocolatey. The town hall's been transformed into a holiday battlefield, tables lined with crooked gingerbread houses, barns with graham-cracker fences, and one very suspect reindeer that looks like it's suffering an existential crisis.

Mharie drifts beside me, arms loosely folded, steps unhurried as she takes in the entries. There's still that keen watchfulness in her eyes, but tonight it feels gentler like she's letting herself enjoy the crooked candy roofs and lopsided gumdrop fences instead of judging them. A faint smile tugs at her mouth when a little girl proudly points out her gingerbread barn, and for the first time since I've been here, Mharie looks less like a woman braced for battle and more like someone who belongs in the middle of all this laughter and sugar.

We stop at one that makes me pause. A gingerbread goat leans sideways, frosting beard drooping like it's been through three rounds with a toddler and lost. Its gumdrop eyes stare at me with familiar menace.

Christ. Emmanuel in cookie form. I bite back a laugh. Back in Willow Glen, that goat would've knocked the table over just for fun, probably eaten half the roof on his way out.

Mharie tips her head, fighting a smile. "Think it'll win?"

"If destruction counts, it's champion material."

She almost laughs, and for a moment, I forget the weight pressing down on both of us. But then a drawl slices through the sugar-sweet air.

"Well, if it ain't our city boy."

Wendell Ray Sutton. Boots polished like he thinks shine makes him respectable, toothpick bobbing in his teeth. His grin spreads as he saunters up, voice loud enough to carry.

"Playin' cowboy, are ya? Everybody in town knows it's a sham. This land don't need some Yankee fiancé from New York. Needs a real Sutton. Needs a real cowboy who can handle Texas dirt."

The crowd goes quiet, just the rustle of candy wrappers and a couple of nervous coughs.

I face him square, calm. "Funny. From where I'm standin', you don't know the first damn thing about Henry's land. You just run your mouth and wait for someone else to do the work. So here's my offer either show up or shut up." Gasps ripple. Wendell's smirk falters, but he recovers quickly, puffing his chest like a bull ready to charge.

Before he can spit something back, a booming voice cuts through.

"Now that sounds like a challenge worth watchin'." Jaxon Walker strides over like a man who already knows exactly what mess he's walking into. Of course he does Walker Ranch touches half the town, and Jaxon knows every rancher, every fence line, and every feud by heart. Baby Candice bounces on his hip, clapping pudgy hands like she knows the drama's good. Taylor trots beside him, little rope slung proudly across his shoulder.

"Evenin', Wendell," Jaxon says, grin easy but edged.

Wendell tips his hat, faking politeness. "Evenin', Jaxon."

"Sounds to me like you're callin' for a cowboy-off," Jaxon says, voice rolling over the crowd. "And truth is, I ain't seen you sit on anything but your own backside in years. Let's settle it properly."

Cheers erupt. A couple of men slap the table; kids squeal. Jaxon raises his voice over the din: "Beto! Junior! Round up some ropers and horses. We're headed to the fairgrounds for a little exhibition!"

The crowd surges, half the town spilling toward the door in a tide of holiday cheer turned bloodsport. Wendell tips his hat like it was his idea all along, though the tight set of his jaw tells the truth.

Beside me, Mharie leans in, voice low. "Careful. Wendell'll try somethin'. He always does."

I give her a steady smile. "Let him."

The fairgrounds glow like an oasis against the dark December sky. Lanterns throw warm circles of light across the arena, the stands filling with townsfolk drifting in from the square. Kids climb rails for a better view, and the smell of hot chocolate mixes with dust in the air. In the ring, riders lope their horses in wide circles, putting them through spins, stops, and tight figure-eights enough showmanship to get the crowd buzzing. The fairgrounds are always ready for a night like this; the Walkers keep this place primed year round.

A ranch hand jogs our way, tack slung over his shoulder. A steady-faced roan mare follows at his hip. He stops in front of me, nodding once. "Logan Richards," he says, offering a hand. "Walker Ranch. We run most of the events out here."

I shake it. "Patrick Williams."

"Figured as much," he replies, tightening the cinch with quick, practiced pulls. "Heard we needed a mount for a little...friendly demonstration." His mouth twitches like he knows exactly how friendly this is. "She'll do right by you. Sure-footed. Quick. Knows her job."

"Appreciate it," I say, swinging into the saddle.

Logan steps back, giving the mare a pat before calling, "Give 'er her head, and she'll take care of the rest. Good luck out there."

"Perfect," I say, swinging into the saddle. The leather creaks, the mare shifting beneath me like she's ready for business.

Wendell mounts up, sloppy, his horse sidestepping under the rough grip. He yanks the reins, earning himself a glare from more than one rancher on the rail. Doesn't faze him. The ropers show off first spinning loops, threading patterns like lace in the air. The crowd oohs and claps. Then the calves are released, one by one.

Wendell goes first. His rope slaps dirt, loops wide, miss after miss. Each failure draws a louder murmur. He growls under his breath, spurs too hard, and jerks his rope cruelly when he finally snags a calf. The animal bawls, stumbling. Mothers near the fence pull their children closer, disapproval etched on their faces.

"Sloppy," a man mutters behind me. "All show, no hand."

When my turn comes, the arena hushes. I ease the mare forward, spin the loop once, twice, then let it fly. Clean. Rope slides snug, calf turned smooth as butter. Dally, turn, done. Simple. Efficient. The crowd bursts into cheers. Taylor whoops from the rail, bouncing like he'll take flight. Another calf. Another clean catch. Faster this time, smoother; the mare is reading my cues like we've worked together for years. Dust plumes gold under the lanterns as I swing wide, loop settling perfectly.

By the third, I'm locked in. Horse steady, rope singing true. We move like one body, rhythm perfect. The calf's caught clean, turned sharp, the whole run faster than the last.

Cheers slam through the arena like thunder. Hats wave, kids scream, and someone whistles sharply enough to split the air.

"New record!" a voice shouts. "Fastest damn run in Piper Falls!"

The weight in my chest shifts. I hadn't realized how much proving myself mattered not until this moment, with the whole town roaring like maybe, just maybe, I belong here. I glance at the rail. Mharie's there, arms tight across her chest, but her eyes... there's something softer in them. Fear, pride, maybe both. She doesn't smile, not fully, but it's enough to pull me straighter in the saddle.

Wendell seethes, face red under the lantern light. He jerks his horse again, rope flying sloppily. The calf stumbles, bawls, and nearly goes down hard.

"Easy, Wendell!" Jaxon's voice cuts sharply, carrying across the arena. "That's a calf, not your temper. You keep takin' it out on the animals, you'll answer to more than me."

The crowd hushes then turns on Wendell with low mutters and shaking heads.

I sit tall, rope coiled neat, mare calm under me. The cheers rise again not just for the roping, but for the difference plain as day.

When it's done, the fairgrounds hum like a festival. Kids chatter, women clap, men nod. Wendell skulks off, jaw tight, muttering under his breath. He's beaten, and the whole damn town knows it.

I ride to the rail where Taylor's bouncing, rope in hand, eyes shining like I just turned water into wine. "That was amazin', Mister Patrick!"

"Stick close to your dad, kiddo," I tell him, handing the rope back. "You'll be ropin' better than me in no time."

Candice claps her tiny hands, gummy smile wide, and the crowd laughs at her enthusiasm. Mharie's still watching me, mouth set in that not-smile. But her eyes linger longer this time, and what I see there nearly knocks the breath out of me. Pride, yes. Relief too. But beneath it something else. Something that looks a whole lot like the same pull I've been fighting since the day I met her.

For a heartbeat, the fairgrounds noise fades. It's just her and me, lantern light glinting in her eyes, and the dawning realization that maybe she's starting to feel it too that same current that's got me so tangled up I can't remember what life looked like without her in it. It warms me more than the lanterns ever could. And it scares me more than Wendell Ray Sutton ever will.

Wendell Ray Sutton who's currently walking away with nothing but dust on his boots.

And me? I've got the town's respect ringing in my ears and the faintest glimmer of hope in Mharie's eyes.

Chapter Sixteen

Mharie

The Cozy Bean glows like a snow globe come to life. Strings of garland and twinkle lights spill warmth across the rafters, catching on the sugar dust that hangs in the air like frost. Heat wraps around me the moment the door shuts, a soft wall against the chill. Every table is crowded with paper plates and bowls of sprinkles, the surfaces sticky from icing mishaps, parchment paper crackling under little hands pressing too hard. It feels messy and alive, like the whole town has squeezed itself into one room to chase Christmas cheer.

Patrick holds the door for me, his shoulder brushing mine as we step inside. He looks around like he's measuring the space, half wary and half amused, while I try not to stare at the way kids swarm the tables like bees at honey.

"Whole lot of sugar," he mutters under his breath.

"Aye," I answer, lips twitching. "And that's before the cookies."

The contest is simple enough: decorate a dozen cookies however you please, with prizes for creativity. But watching Piper Falls at it, you'd think it was a high-stakes rodeo. Mothers and fathers huddle over bowls of frosting, some children concentrating hard, others licking their fingers without shame. Laughter bounces off the walls, and for a heartbeat, I let myself enjoy it, this messy, ordinary chaos.

Taylor Walker beams when he spots Patrick. "Mr. Patrick! Come help me!"

Before I can blink, Patrick is crouched at the boy's side, steadying Taylor's small hand as he pipes a shaky star. Patrick's voice is low and patient, the kind of quiet instruction that sinks into a person rather than hovers over them. It hits something deep in my chest. I've seen him be steady, practical, unflinching when things go wrong, but watching him teach a child with this much care feels like seeing a door I didn't realize he had.

It shouldn't surprise me, but it does. There's a softness in him that he rarely shows on purpose, and it tugs at me in ways I'm not ready to name.

Baby Candice claps from Jaxon's arms, sticky palms smearing his shirt, and the whole table erupts in giggles. Even Patrick smiles, real and unguarded, and the sight warms me more than the cocoa cups lined along the counter.

"Looks like you've found yourself a natural," Ms. Walker teases from across the table. "Careful, Mharie. A man good with kids is a dangerous thing."

Before I can fire back, two older women from church lean in, voices sweet as honey and just as sticky.

"Such a handsome pair," one croons.

"Bet you'll have little ones of your own by next Christmas," the other adds, winking like she's handing out blessings.

Heat rushes up my neck. "We're—"

Patrick cuts in smooth as silk. "Appreciate the confidence, ma'am."

I glance at him, startled, but he doesn't flinch. He doesn't even blink. He just keeps guiding Taylor's hand like the whole town isn't watching me blush crimson.

The contest ends in a flurry of sprinkles and applause. A little girl with frosting up to her elbows takes the prize, her gingerbread cow somehow managing to stand upright. Everyone cheers as though she's won a blue ribbon at the county fair. Mrs. Tate presses a bakery box of "extras" into my hands as we head for the door.

Outside the night air nips at my cheeks, sharp after the heat of the café. Patrick unlocks the truck, holding the box while I climb in. We drive in companionable quiet, Main Street fading behind us in a trail of garland-lit windows and muffled carols.

"Handled yourself well," he says after a while, eyes still on the road.

"Barely." I laugh softly. "Those women should be armed with warning signs."

His mouth curves. "Not my first rodeo."

The road unspools dark and silver. With every mile, the buzz of sugar and noise slips away, leaving something quieter between us.

At the homestead, the porch light glows against the frost. Dougal bellows from the paddock, offended as always at our lateness. Patrick carries the bakery box in and sets it on the counter while I hang up my coat.

"You hungry?" he asks.

I nod. "We could raid the cookie box."

He lifts a brow. "Make it official? Spiked eggnog and stolen cookies?"

"I've got Henry's old recipe," I say, tugging open the cabinet for nutmeg and cream. "He swore it'd put hair on your chest."

Patrick chuckles low. "Guess we'll test that theory."

We work side by side in the kitchen, sleeves pushed up, steam curling from mugs as I whisk and he pours. Our elbows brush once, then again, each time lingering a heartbeat longer. By the time we carry the drinks into the living room, the air between us is as warm and fuzzy as the eggnog itself.

The tree still leans in the corner, bare except for a string of lights we draped over it days ago and never finished. Patrick sets the mugs down. "Should probably trim it before it dries out completely."

I fetch the box of ornaments from Henry's closet. We kneel on the rug, pulling out tissue-wrapped memories: wooden stars, glass balls, a lopsided angel made by some long-ago 4-H kid. Patrick hands me the hooks while I describe each one. His big hands look out of place holding such delicate things, but he handles them with care. We hang in silence for a while. Then, without thinking, I lift onto my toes to reach a high branch. My balance wobbles, and his hand comes to my waist, steady and warm. He doesn't drop it right away.

His hand stays there longer than it needs to. Long enough for warmth to seep through Henry's old sweater. Long enough for something inside me to loosen that I didn't realize was clenched.

"Sorry," he murmurs, though he doesn't pull away. His thumb brushes a slow arc just above my hip, barely there and barely intentional, and the breath I'd been holding slips out in a shiver.

"It's alright," I whisper. Too soft. Too honest.

He studies my face like he's solving a puzzle he's been carrying around for weeks. The tree lights flicker gold across his eyes, warm and steady, and suddenly there's no distance left to pretend with.

"I didn't think…" I begin, then stop, because saying it feels like handing him my pulse.

"What?" he asks, voice low and meant only for me.

"I didn't think I'd have space for anything like this. Not now. Not here."

His breath catches, quiet but unmistakable.

"Mharie," he says, my name a rough promise.

I turn my head. Our faces are inches apart. His eyes are dark and intense, not asking, not taking, just waiting. Filled with the promise of something more.

My heart beats so hard I'm sure he can feel it under his hand. I should step back. Instead, I whisper, "Patrick…"

It's the only invitation he needs.

He leans in slow, giving me every chance to stop him. When our mouths meet, it's warm and soft at first, then deepens, hungry enough to make my knees go weak. His fingers slide from my waist up my back, beneath the hem of my sweater, skin to skin, and I gasp into his mouth, feeling the electricity of his touch.

His other hand finds the small of my back, pulling me closer and pressing me against him. I can feel the hard lines of his body, the heat radiating from him, and it makes my head spin. His mouth moves expertly over mine, tasting, exploring, demanding a response I can't deny.

I let my hands roam, feeling the muscles of his shoulders, the strength in his arms, the way his body tenses under my touch. He groans, a sound that makes my knees weak, and desire surges through me.

Without breaking the kiss, he guides me backward, his strong hands steadying me as we stumble against the couch.

I fall back, pulling him with me, my legs wrapping around his waist without thinking as we sink into the soft cushions. He settles on top of me, his weight both grounding and exhilarating.

His hands explore my body, tracing the curve of my hip, the swell of my breast, sending shivers of anticipation through me. I arch into his touch, wanting more, needing more. His mouth leaves mine, trailing hot kisses down my neck, his stubble rough against sensitive skin.

I can feel his heart pounding against my chest, matching the frantic rhythm of my own. His hands find the edge of my sweater and slowly lift it, his fingers brushing against my skin, setting it alight. I help him, eager to feel his touch, his heat, his everything.

Just as his hands reach the clasp of my bra, a thud rattles the back door. Dougal's head appears in the window, shaggy and ridiculous, snorting at us like a chaperone. We break apart, laughing breathlessly, foreheads almost touching.

"Guess that's our cue," Patrick murmurs, his thumb brushing my jaw before he lets go.

I step back, chest rising and falling. "Spiked eggnog might've been a mistake."

"Best mistake I've made in a long time," he says quietly.

We finish the tree with trembling hands and too much laughter, but the air between us has changed. Warmer. Charged. A door opened that neither of us can close again.

Patrick

The smell of coffee is what gets me moving, but it's not what I reach for. Mharie's at the counter, hair loose around her shoulders, fingers curled around the tin of sugar when I lean in and kiss her. Not gentle. Not tentative. Just something that's been simmering under my ribs finally breaking the surface. She stiffens for a second. Then softens, warm and willing, her hand curling against my chest like she's trying to decide whether to push me away or pull me closer. I don't know which I want more myself.

She tastes like sleep and heat and whatever part of her I've been trying not to want too much. The kettle whistles. She startles and steps back, breath unsteady, cheeks flushed. That shy little pull at the corner of her mouth nearly takes my legs out. She pours the hot water over her tea while I fill two mismatched mugs with coffee like we've been doing this for years. Her eyes keep flicking to mine, hazy from the kiss, and there's a question hovering between us neither of us is brave enough to voice yet.

I hand her the mug. Our fingers brush. Sparks, again. She takes a slow sip, studying me over the rim, and I can't help wondering if she's replaying that kiss the way I am—if she's wondering what it would feel like to pick up where we left off.

Then.....crunch.

Gravel under tires. Slow. Heavy. Too close to be a passerby.

We freeze. Mharie straightens her coat. I swipe a hand over my mouth like that'll hide anything from anyone.

Then comes the bellow. Deep. Guttural. Offended.

Dougal.

We both move to the window. A delivery man sits stiff as a fence post in the cab of a truck, eyes wide as Dougal plants himself in front of the bumper like a furry troll demanding a toll.

"Guess that box is mine," I mutter, already fighting a grin.

Mharie exhales, half exasperation, half laughter she tries to hide. "Better you than me."

She's still pink from the kiss. And I'm still burning from it.

But the moment breaks cleanly, *not ruined, not repeated*, just delayed, while Dougal snorts steam at a terrified man who clearly didn't expect his Tuesday to include a face-off with a Highland cow.

And honestly?

I don't mind the interruption. Because the way her eyes linger on me before she turns toward the mudroom tells me one thing clear as sky

By midmorning, the house hums with more than caffeine. Boxes are stacked on the porch two extra regulators, a fresh batch of eight trail cams, backup batteries, even a compact solar array. More equipment than I originally planned. More than we strictly need.

But after the last few days? Necessary.

I toe one of the boxes closer with my boot, jaw tightening. One gate latch bent out of shape. A fresh set of boot prints in the east pasture that didn't match ours. Nothing big. Nothing dramatic. Nothing I can prove.

But enough.

Enough to tell me Wendell, or someone working for him, is circling closer than he wants the county to know. Enough that I'm not leaving this place blind, not for a single minute.

"These're new," Mharie says quietly, tapping a finger against one of the sealed boxes.

"They'll give us eyes on every fence line," I answer. "Back pasture too. And the creek cut. If anything shifts, we'll know."

She nods, worry tight behind her eyes, then steadies herself. "Aye. Let's get them up."

We do the rest together because this land deserves more than fear, and she deserves more than standing alone in the dark. I start with the water regulators, crouched at the pump while cold bites through my gloves. A simple fix, but it'll stretch every gallon and keep the troughs steady when the pipes freeze. Mharie stands nearby with her arms tucked around herself, watching like she wants to ask questions but bites them back.

"Nothing fancy," I tell her, tightening the last coupling. "Just means the cattle don't go thirsty if the lines run slow."

She nods, the kind of nod that says she understands more than she lets on. The panels come next. I haul them up to the shed roof, angle them toward the sharp winter sun. Not much daylight in December, but enough to feed the batteries and give her some independence from the grid. I glance down once, catch her holding the ladder steady, face tipped up toward me.

The trail cams take the longest. We walk the fence line together, boots crunching frost, her carrying the bag of straps while I mount each camera high on cedar posts. She teases me for fussing over angles, but she doesn't complain. Not when both of us know Wendell already has eyes on this land. Better for us to have our own.

When the last one clicks into place, I brush dirt from my gloves. "Won't stop him from trying something," I say. "But it means we'll know."

Her answer is soft, steady. "And that means we'll be ready."

Something twists in my chest. I'm not just setting up equipment. I'm putting down roots. The rest of the day is lighter. I split firewood, sweat soaking through my flannel, while she laughs at Dougal's attempts to chew the catch the tassels on her hat. She strokes Dougal's shaggy neck while I scatter hay, her smile soft enough to quiet every doubt I've been carrying.

By the time the sun dips low, the place feels... different. Stronger. Ours. I want to kiss her again. God, I want more than that. The air between us hums with it, and I don't care if the whole damn county guesses what's happening here. Dougal barrels in, his horns catching the edge of a cardboard box on the porch, nearly sending it tumbling. The moment dissolves in laughter. She swats at him, muttering in that musical brogue, and I steady the box before it spills across the floor.

When I straighten, she's watching me. No sharpness. No guarded distance. Just pride. Trust. And something warmer something that makes me think maybe this whole fake fiancé act isn't feeling so fake anymore. I step closer. Close enough that if I reached for her, if I just tipped my head, the space between us would vanish.

And maybe it should.

Mharie's breath hitches as I close the distance, her eyes fluttering closed as my lips brush against hers. The kiss deepens, becoming more urgent, more demanding. My hands find her waist, pulling her flush against me, and she responds with a soft moan that vibrates through my chest. Her fingers tangle in my hair, holding me close, as if she's afraid I might pull away. But I have no intention of stopping. Not now. Not when every nerve in my body is alight with desire.

I trail kisses down her jaw, feeling her pulse race beneath my lips. Her head falls back, exposing her neck, and I take the invitation, nipping and sucking at the delicate skin. Her breath comes in ragged gasps, and I can feel her heart pounding against my chest. My hands roam, eagerly exploring the curves of her body, and she arches into my touch, encouraging me. The room spins around me, the world narrowing down to just the two of us, lost in a tangle of limbs.

But just as things start to escalate further, I pull back, my eyes searching hers. "Mharie," I whisper, my voice hoarse with desire, "are you sure about this? Do you really want this?"

Her eyes meet mine, dark with passion, and a slow smile spreads across her face. "Aye," she breathes, her voice barely audible. "I'm sure."

With that, I take her hand and lead her toward the stairs, the anticipation building with every step. We don't get far before I pull her into my arms once more, ready to explore every inch of her, to lose myself in her completely. I push her gently against the wall, my body pressing against hers, and she gasps as I capture her lips in a searing kiss. My hands slide under her shirt, lifting it off her slowly, feeling the soft skin of her back, and she shivers beneath my touch. I can't help the moan that slips out. I trail kisses down her neck, my teeth grazing her collarbone, and her head falls back against the wall, allowing me more access to her warm skin.

She tugs at my shirt, pulling it over my head, and I oblige, eager to feel her skin against mine. My fingers find the clasp of her bra, and with a flick, it falls away, leaving her bare to my gaze. I take a moment to appreciate the sight of her, her breasts heaving with each ragged breath, before I lean down and capture one nipple in my mouth. She cries out, her fingers digging into my shoulders, and I lavish attention on her, my tongue swirling around the sensitive peak. My hand trails down her stomach, slipping beneath the waistband of her pants, and she bucks against my touch, urging me on.

I slide a finger inside her, feeling her wet and ready, and she moans, her hips moving in time with my strokes. I add another finger, stretching her, preparing her, and she gasps, her body clenching around me.

"More," she whispers, her voice hoarse with desire. "I need more."

I oblige, my thumb finding her clit, rubbing in tight circles as my fingers continue to pump in and out of her. She cries out, her body tensing, and I can feel her getting close. I capture her lips in a searing kiss, swallowing her moans as she comes undone in my arms. Her body shakes with the force of her orgasm, and I hold her close, my heart pounding in my chest. I know this is just the beginning, and I'm ready to explore every inch of her, to lose myself in her completely.

Chapter Eighteen

Mharie

We barely make it up the stairs. Every step feels like a decision we're making together, breathless and certain, shedding hesitation the way we shed coats and layers. By the time my back bumps the bedroom door, we're not starting something new we're picking up the thread we dropped last night, the one that's been tugging between us for days. We barely pause long enough for the latch to catch before he's guiding me backward, step by slow step.

His mouth claims mine like he's been waiting a lifetime. My fingers slide into his hair, tugging him closer, and he groans low and rough, the kind of sound that vibrates straight through me. Heat sparks under my skin. My knees go weak. The backs of my legs hit the mattress. He pauses just long enough to search my face. Just long enough to give me a chance to change my mind.

I don't.

I curl my hand around the back of his neck and whisper, "Aye." Before removing my sweater and tossing it to the floor and sliding my jeans down my legs.

It's all the permission he needs, his clothes join mine on the floor.

He kisses me again, deeper this time, guiding me backward until I'm lying against the pillows and he's braced above me, his weight warm and solid between my thighs. His fingertips trace my ribs, my waist, the sensitive dip just above my hip. Every touch leaves fire in its wake. He's there, mouth trailing heat across the top of my chest, down the center, reverent and greedy all at once. I arch into him without thinking, desperate for more. His name catches in my throat, a broken sound.

"God, Mharie..." he murmurs against my skin, and the way he says it makes my pulse stumble.

My hands roam over his shoulders, the strong line of his back, his warm skin. He leans down to kiss me again, breath unsteady. We sink into the mattress together, bodies aligning like they've done this a hundred times. And then his hand slides lower.

Slow. Intentional. Certain.

My breath stutters. My legs fall open for him without a second thought. And when his fingers find me already aching, already wet for him I gasp into his mouth, the sound swallowed by his kiss.

This time, I don't hold back.

I gasp again, clutching at his hair, his shoulders, anything to keep me tethered to reality. My body moves of its own accord, shameless in its need, grinding against his hand. I've kissed men before, aye, but never like this, never with my whole body shaking, never with my soul screaming yes even while my mind tries to catch up.

"Patrick," I whisper, and he looks at me like I'm the only woman in the world. Like I'm home.

The thought undoes me more than his touch. I come apart in his arms, trembling, clinging to him as the world tilts and spins. His lips find mine again, softer this time, as if he knows I need the sweetness as much as the fire. The bedframe creaks as Patrick shifts, and I hear the thud of boots hitting the floor. Then his skin is immediately against mine, hot and smooth, rough with scars and calluses. I feel both wicked and wanted, cherished and consumed. His mouth trails down my chest, worshipful and greedy in equal measure, nipping and sucking at my sensitive skin. I arch beneath him, helpless to do anything but give, my body a willing sacrifice to his touch.

His hands map my curves, tracing the dip of my waist, the flare of my hips, the soft skin of my inner thighs. I shiver under his touch, my breath coming in ragged gasps. When his fingers find my center, sliding inside me, I cry out, my body clenching around him, desperate for more.

"Please," I breathe, the word raw and desperate in my throat. "More. I need more."

His answering growl vibrates through me, a promise of what's to come. When he slides inside, filling me slow and steady, I forget every reason I ever had to leave this place. He stretches me, fills me completely, and I wrap my legs around him, urging him deeper. The rhythm builds, a firestorm in the dark, our bodies moving in perfect sync. I lose myself in him in the way he whispers my name like a vow, in the way his body moves with mine, in the way he doesn't hold back. His hips thrust against mine, hard and fast, and I meet him stroke for stroke, my nails digging into his back, marking him as mine.

When it comes again, the release tears through me like lightning, searing and intense. I cling to him, nails biting into his shoulders, knowing I'll never be the same. My body shakes with the force of my orgasm, and he follows soon after, his body tensing, his release spilling into me, hot and pulsing.

Later, when the storm passes and we're tangled in sheets, sweat cooling on my skin, I look at him. Really look. His chest rises and falls, his eyes still fierce, even softened by exhaustion. A sheen of sweat glistens on his skin, and I reach out, tracing the lines of his body, the strength in him, the man who keeps showing up when he doesn't have to.

And in that moment, the truth slams into me harder than any kiss.

This man isn't just my pretend fiancé. He isn't just a way to keep Henry's land safe. He's becoming mine whether I meant it or not. His hand reaches out, tracing the curve of my hip, the swell of my breast, and I shiver at his touch. The room is quiet, the only sound our mingled breaths and the occasional creak of the old bed frame. I can feel the weight of his gaze, the intensity of his stare, and it makes my heart race.

"I've wanted this for so long," he says, his voice low and rough. "You have no idea how much I've wanted you."

I turn to face him, propping myself up on one elbow, my fingers tracing the lines of his face, the stubble rough against my skin. "And I've been fighting it," I admit, my voice barely a whisper. "Fighting the way ye make me feel."

He grins, a wicked glint in his eye, and pulls me closer, his body pressing against mine. "Then stop fighting," he murmurs, his lips brushing against my ear. "Because I'm not letting you go."

I can feel the hardness of him, already stirring against my thigh, and I gasp, my body responding instantly. His hands roam my body, exploring every curve, every inch of skin, and I arch into his touch, urging him on.

He rolls me onto my back, his body covering mine, and I wrap my legs around him, pulling him closer. I can feel the heat of him, the need, and it matches my own. His lips capture mine in a searing kiss, and I melt into him, my fingers tangling in his hair, pulling him closer. His hands slide down my body, finding the wetness between my thighs, and he groans, his fingers sliding inside me, stretching me, preparing me. I cry out, my body clenching around him, and he captures my lips in a searing kiss, swallowing my moans.

"Patrick," I whisper, my voice hoarse with desire. "I need ye. Now."

He positions himself at my entrance, and with one swift thrust, he's inside me, filling me completely. I cry out, my body stretching to accommodate him, and he stills, giving me a moment to adjust.

"You okay?" he asks, his voice a low growl, his eyes searching mine.

"Aye," I breathe, my voice barely audible. "Dinnae stop."

He grins, a wicked glint in his eye, and begins to move, his hips thrusting against mine. I meet his every movement, my body arching against his, and we find a rhythm, a dance that's as old as time.

His hands are everywhere, exploring my body, his lips capturing mine in searing kisses. I can feel myself getting close, my body tensing, and he must sense it too, because he reaches between us, his thumb finding my clit, rubbing in tight circles.

I cry out, my body clenching around him, and he groans, his head falling to my shoulder. I can feel him, hard and pulsing inside me, and I know he's close too.

"I'm right there," he groans, his forehead pressed to mine. "Come with me. Don't hold back." And with those words, I do. I let go, my body shaking with the force of my orgasm, and he follows soon after, his body tensing, his release spilling into me, hot and pulsing.

We lay there, our bodies entwined, our breaths mingling, and I know this is just the beginning. I'm ready to explore every inch of him, to lose myself in him completely.

But as his arms tighten around me, as steady and warm as the Texas night, a sliver of unease slips in. Because come January, I'm meant to be in Scotland, chasing the future I've fought tooth and nail for. The trouble is, lying here, wrapped up in him, the homestead feels every bit as much mine as the heathered hills of Glencoe ever did.

And for the first time, I wonder if the decision I thought was so clear-cut might tear me in two.

Chapter Nineteen

Patrick

Morning settles over the homestead soft and quiet, but everything between us feels different. Not because of the town because of last night.

Mharie and I move around the kitchen like we've been doing this for years bumping shoulders, sharing grins, stealing quick touches when she passes me the butter or I set a mug by her hand. There's no edge, no pretending. Just... us.

By midmorning, we're out in the pastures, bundled against the cold, tackling chores side by side. The sky's pale, the kind of winter blue that looks too thin to hold. Frost crunches under our boots, and our breath clouds the air as we walk the fence line. She finds a stretch of wire loose again. Too neat to be weather and too careless to be Henry, someone wanted it found. Not broken, not trampled... just wrong. Wrong in a way that puts a tight pulse behind my jaw. Accidents happen on ranches, sure, but this feels like a warning left in plain sight.

Two calves dropped in the night. Tiny, knobby-kneed, and wobbly as they nose around their mothers. Mharie's face softens like I've never seen before, her hand clutched tight around mine as we watch them totter. I tuck that image away, knowing I'll carry it for the rest of my life.

It hits me harder than I expect this small, quiet moment that feels like the start of something solid.

Later, when I'm pitching hay in the barn, my phone buzzes. Adam.

I duck into the tack room to hear him better, though Dougal lumbers in after me, crowding the space with his shaggy bulk like he's got every right to be part of the call.

"'Bout damn time," Adam says when I answer. "Nessa made it to New York yesterday. Christiane's already in love."

The grin in his voice is contagious, and I find myself smiling even as Dougal noses the phone, nearly knocking it from my hand. "That's great, man. She'll fit right in."

"Yeah, if we can keep her from following Christiane around like a shadow." Adam chuckles. "Anyway, what's that racket? Sounds like a damn tuba in the background."

I glance at Dougal, who's decided the door jamb is his personal scratching post. "That'd be Dougal. Think Emmanuel, but with more horns and less sense."

Adam howls with laughter. "You're telling me you've got an overgrown Emmanuel down there? Man, I gotta see this."

"Trust me, he's impossible to miss." Dougal swings his head, nearly knocking over a shovel, and I shove him back with my boot. He just huffs at me like I'm the one in his way.

Adam calms enough to tease, "Sounds like you're getting pretty settled, though. You gonna admit it? Texas starting to feel permanent?"

I lean against the stall door, watching Mharie through the slats as she brushes down one of the mares. My chest tightens. "Yeah," I admit. "It is. But the future's still... uncertain. A lot of moving pieces."

"Want me to come down? You know I can get there quick." His tone sharpens, protective like always.

I shake my head, though he can't see it. "No. I've got it. Just need to hold the line for a while."

There's a pause, then Adam sighs. "Alright. But don't you dare try to do it all alone if it gets heavy. You hear me?"

"Loud and clear," I say, smiling at the same time. Mharie glances over, catching my eye. She smiles back, soft and certain, like she already knows the choice I'm too stubborn to make.

Dougal chooses that moment to bellow loud enough to rattle the roof beams. Adam's laughter booms through the line before he hangs up, and I swear the big shaggy beast grins.

By the time the sun slips low, painting the pasture gold, we're both worn through. Our boots are caked, our cheeks raw from the wind, but we're laughing as we stomp up the porch steps. The kind of laugh that comes easy after a day done right.

Inside, the kitchen smells like rosemary and garlic. Mharie hums as she chops, swaying a little, while I set the skillet on the stove. We work shoulder to shoulder, trading utensils, brushing past each other in the small space. Every touch sparks, every glance lingers.

"Careful," she says when my hand brushes hers on the knife handle.

"Just trying to help."

"Mm-hm," she mutters, but there's a smile tugging at her lips.

I take the dare. "I've got steady hands."

"Overconfident New Yorker," she mutters, but there's a smile tugging at her lips.

Even as we cook, my mind keeps circling back to that fence line the wire loosened clean, deliberate. It hangs between us, unspoken but real, like a draft slipping through a closed door. Whoever touched that fence didn't come by accident. But right now, with her laughter warming the kitchen, I let it sit at the edge of the room. Dinner is simple pan-seared chicken, roasted carrots, a bottle of red she pulled from Henry's stash, but it feels like a feast. We eat at the small table, knees bumping, laughter spilling easily between bites. She tells me about summers here as a girl, riding fence lines with Henry and learning the history of the land. I tell her about winters back home in Willow Glen, frozen pipes, and how Adam always took the hardest jobs himself. It's so ordinary and it's everything.

When the plates are pushed aside and the bottle is nearly empty, I reach across, brushing her hand with mine. "Come here."

Her breath catches, but she doesn't hesitate. She comes to me, and the kiss is hungry from the start all the pretending finally burning off. She tastes like wine and rosemary, like every good thing I never thought I'd have. Her fingers curl into my shirt, pulling me closer until there's no space left to close.

We stumble back toward the counter, laughter mixing with heat. She breaks away long enough to whisper, "This isn't wise."

"Maybe not," I murmur against her throat. "But it's real."

Her only answer is a soft sound as I lift her onto the counter, her legs curling around me, her hair brushing my cheek as she leans in again. Her lips find mine, urgent and demanding, and I respond with a growl, my hands roaming her body, exploring every curve, every inch of skin.

I push her shirt up, exposing her smooth stomach, and she gasps as my lips trail down, nipping and sucking at her sensitive skin. Her hands tangle in my hair, holding me close, urging me on. I can feel the heat of her, the need, and it matches my own.

I slide my hands beneath her, lifting her easily, and she wraps her legs around me, her arms around my neck. I carry her to the bedroom, aching with desire, my lips never leaving hers. I lay her down on the bed, my body covering hers, and she arches up against me, pressing into me.

I take a moment to appreciate the sight of her, her hair spread out on the pillow, her eyes dark with passion, her cheeks flushed with desire. She reaches for me, pulling me down, her lips capturing mine in a searing kiss. I can feel the hardness of her nipples against my chest, the softness of her skin, the heat of her body.

I trail kisses down her neck, my teeth nipping at her collarbone, and she moans, her head falling back. I slide my hand beneath her shirt and she leans forward as we work together to remove it. Finding the clasp of her bra next, it falls away with a flick of my fingers, leaving her bare to my gaze. I take a moment to appreciate the sight of her, her breasts heaving with each ragged breath, before I lean down and capture one nipple in my mouth.

She cries out, her fingers digging into my shoulders, and I lavish attention on her, my tongue swirling around the sensitive peak. My hand slides down her body, finding the waistband of her pants, and I quickly undo the button, pushing them down, taking her underwear with them. She lifts her hips, helping me, and I can see the wetness between her thighs, the evidence of her desire.

I slide my hand between her legs, feeling her wet and ready, and she bucks against my touch, urging me on. I slide two fingers inside her, pumping in and out, stretching her, preparing her, and she cries out, her body moving in time with my strokes.

"Patrick," she whispers, her voice hoarse with desire. "I need you. Now."

I position myself at her entrance, and with one swift thrust, I'm inside her, filling her completely, and it's all I can do not to lose myself with her heat. Mharie cries out, her body stretching to accommodate me, and I hold for just a moment, giving her time to adjust. Then her legs wrap around me, urging me deeper, and I begin to move, my hips thrusting against hers, one finger circling her clit and driving us both higher.

The rhythm builds, a firestorm in the dark, our bodies moving in perfect sync. I lose myself in her in the way she whispers my name like a vow, in the way her body moves with mine, in the way she doesn't hold back. Her nails dig into my back, marking me as hers, and I can feel myself getting close, my body tensing, my release building.

"Come with me," I growl, my voice hoarse with desire. "Let go."

And with those words, she does. Her body shakes with the force of her orgasm, and I can't hold back anymore, my body tensing, my release spilling into her, hot and pulsing. We lay there, limbs entwined, breaths mingling, and I know this is just the beginning.

I roll off her, pulling her into my arms, her back to my chest, and she snuggles close, her body fitting perfectly against mine. I can feel her heart beating, her breath slow and steady, and I know she's mine whether she meant it or not.

The rest of the world Wendell, the town, the homestead's uncertain future falls away until there's only us.

Chapter Twenty

Mharie

I wake before the alarm, cocooned in warmth. Patrick's arm is heavy across my waist, his breath a steady puff at the back of my neck. My muscles ache in ways I didn't know they could, but it's a good ache—deep, satisfying, a reminder of everything we gave each other last night.

I shift slightly, and his grip tightens, his hand sliding over my stomach, fingers splaying possessively. "Don't move yet," he murmurs, voice still rough from sleep. "Five more minutes."

His palm drifts lower, a slow, lazy stroke over my hip that makes my pulse jump. Heat curls low in my belly. He presses a kiss to my shoulder, then another just below my ear. "You okay?" he asks quietly.

I turn to face him, my hand on his chest. "Aye," I whisper. "More than okay."

His eyes search mine, still dark from sleep but already sparking. He dips his head, capturing my mouth in a slow kiss that turns deeper, hotter, until I'm melting against him again. His fingers slide under the hem of the oversized shirt I threw on sometime in the night, finding bare skin, tracing circles that make me tremble.

"Patrick..." My voice breaks on his name.

He smiles against my mouth, a wicked curve that makes me ache. "Sun's already up," he murmurs against my lips, sounding anything but motivated. "We should get movin'."

"I dinnae think either of us is in a rush," I whisper, brushing my mouth over his, giving him the answer he's really looking for.

His laugh rumbles against my throat, low and delighted, before he rolls me beneath him. "Careful what you offer, sweetheart."

I push him back, a playful shove, before shifting to straddle him, my knees on either side of his hips. I slip my shirt over my head and his hands find my waist, thumbs brushing the underside of my breasts, making me shiver. I lean down, capturing his mouth, my tongue tasting him, claiming him.

He groans, his hands sliding up my back, pulling me closer, his hardness pressing against me. I grind against him, feeling him through the thin fabric of his boxers, and he bucks his hips, meeting my every movement. His lips trail down my neck, nipping and sucking at my sensitive skin, and I gasp, my head tipping back.

I sit up, my hands finding the waistband of his boxers, and push them down, freeing him. He lifts his hips, helping me, and I take a moment to appreciate the sight of him, hard and ready for me. I wrap my hand around him, feel the pulse of him in my grip, and he groans, his head falling back to the pillow.

I position myself over him, feeling the head of him at my entrance, and slowly lower myself, taking him inch by inch. He fills me completely, stretching me, and I moan, my body clenching around him. He reaches up, his hands cupping my breasts, thumbs brushing over my nipples, and I arch into his touch, needing more.

I move, hips rolling as I find a rhythm that has us both gasping. Patrick's hands grip my hips, guiding me, his body meeting mine stroke for stroke. I lean forward, my palms braced on his chest for balance, and he lifts his head, catching one of my nipples in his mouth, sucking and nipping until sparks shoot straight through me.

"Patrick," I whisper, voice hoarse with need. "You feel... so good."

He looks up at me, eyes dark and hungry, a wicked glint in them. "So do you, sweetheart. Don't stop."

So I don't. I ride him with a wild abandon that would've scared me weeks ago, chasing the pleasure building inside me. His hands roam my body, mapping every curve, every shiver, and I tremble under his touch.

I can feel myself getting close, my body tightening around him, and he feels it too. One of his hands slips between us, his thumb finding my clit, circling in tight, devastating strokes.

I cry out, my body clenching around him. Patrick groans, his hips jerking up, his release spilling into me, hot and pulsing, as I shatter around him. The world narrows to heat and breath and his name on my lips. I collapse forward, my body shaking with the force of it. Strong arms wrap around me, holding me close. For a moment we just lie there, our bodies entwined, our breaths slowly finding the same rhythm. Eventually, I roll off him, snuggling into his side, my head on his chest, listening to the steady beat of his heart. He pulls the covers over us, his arm wrapping around me, holding me close.

"We're gonna miss the parade if we don't move," I manage, still flushed.

He groans and flings an arm over his eyes. "Worth it."

I swat his chest and, after another stolen minute, slide out of bed, my legs still wobbly. "Get up, New Yorker. The cattle will no' feed themselves."

We dress fast, the quiet between us comfortable, full of glances that say more than words. Every time I catch his eye, heat flickers low in my belly, but there's something steadier under it too. Something that feels dangerously like hope.

Outside, frost glitters like crushed glass on the pasture. The sky is that pale winter blue again, but the world feels sharper, clearer, as if something has been peeled back. Patrick falls into step beside me as we head for the barn, boots crunching in unison. I'm still replaying the way he smiled up at me, the way his hands knew my body like they'd been waiting for it, when something in the distance catches my eye. A dark slash against the pale boards of the far fence. Spray paint.

I stop dead, the cold suddenly biting straight through my coat. Footprints scar the frost, looping around the barn. Heavy boot marks that don't belong to either of us. The paint drips fresh down the wood—letters jagged and uneven, slapped across Henry's boards like a wound.

THIEVES.

The word screams back at me in red.

"Patrick," I call softly, though my throat feels raw.

He follows my gaze, his body going still. Whatever warmth was in his eyes a heartbeat ago hardens to steel. He strides closer, jaw tight, fingertips brushing the still-tacky paint.

"Fresh," he mutters. "Could've been done hours ago."

He glances up toward the nearest post. "Trail cam's pointed straight at this stretch," he says, already reaching for his phone. "If they came through here, we'll see exactly who it was."

I swallow, rage bubbling hot beneath the cold. "On Henry's land. On our land. They've nae right." My voice trembles, but not with fear—with fury.

Patrick turns, scanning the fence line, his shoulders coiled like he expects Wendell himself to come strutting out of the frost. "He wanted you to wake up to this," Patrick says, his voice flat. "Not the town. Just you. He wants you shaken before he makes his next move."

"Same as the wire yesterday," I say, heat rising in my chest. "He's pokin' at the edges first. Testing what we'll tolerate."

My fists clench at my sides. The afterglow from last night is gone, replaced by the bitter taste of violation. I can still feel Patrick's hands on my skin, his warmth wrapped around me, but now it mixes with something sharp and cold. The footprints circle the barn, stop at the corner, then vanish into the field. Patrick crouches, tracing one with his glove. "Heavy step. Same size, repeating. One man, maybe two. They weren't hiding it."

I bite back a curse, Gaelic thick on my tongue. "Wendell thinks to scare me. To shame me. He'll nae win."

Patrick rises, tall against the pale sky, eyes hard as flint. "No," he says, his voice low and final. "He won't."

Right now, the town will be stringing garland and queuing for the parade. Bells will ring, kids will laugh, cocoa will steam in paper cups. But all I can see is the word slashed across our fence.

The fight we thought we had time to ease into is standing on our doorstep.

Chapter Twenty-One

Patrick

We make our way back inside, mud still on our boots, I flip open the laptop on the kitchen table. The footage loads—grainy and washed in cold moonlight.

Empty fence. Then movement. A hooded figure steps into view, turning just enough for the side angle to catch a sliver of his boots—square-toed, ostrich leather, faint teal stitching.

My pulse spikes. "I know those boots."

Mharie leans closer, her breath catching. "Wendell."

"Maybe," I say, though the word tastes like a lie. "He knew where the camera was. Stayed out of its path on purpose." The figure moves with practiced ease, never showing his face. Never offering the camera a clean shot. He sprays the word in one fast pass, then disappears into the frost-dark field.

Mharie's hands curl into fists. "He doesna' even try tae hide it."

"He's taunting us," I say, closing the laptop softly. "But legally? It's a shadow. Could be him, could be anyone with fancy boots."

She swallows hard, shoulders tight, eyes burning with the stubborn fire I've come to admire and fear in equal measure.

"We'll show Mick," I tell her. "He said proof matters."

She nods, but her jaw is set like stone. "Then let him see it."

I touch her elbow gently. "Come on. The parade starts soon."

The bells of the parade are already tolling when we roll into town, the old Chevy rattling like it's as nervous as we are. Mharie sits beside me, her braid tight, jaw tighter, and I can still feel the tremor in her when she stared at that red paint on the barn this morning. I damn near had to drag her back from marching to Wendell's doorstep then and there. Now she's bristling in the passenger seat, and I know if Wendell shows his face, she'll let loose in the middle of Main Street.

"Breathe," I murmur.

Her head snaps toward me. "Dinnae tell me tae breathe." Her accent cuts sharper when she's angry, words like stones skipping on water. "He's mocked Henry's land. Our land."

I reach across the cab and cover her hand where it's white-knuckled on her knee. "And he wants you good and riled before the parade starts. Don't give him the show."

Her lips press tight, but she doesn't pull away. The square is already packed, garlands strung from lamppost to lamppost, a brass band warming up on the courthouse steps. Kids chase one another between boots and hay bales while mamas scold them to sit still for the parade. Folks wave as we pass, but I see the way their eyes flicker, whispers starting in our wake.

They've heard. Of course they have. Piper Falls talks faster than wildfire in August. And there he is: Wendell Ray Sutton, leaning against the feed store porch rail like he owns the whole damn town, hat tipped back, grin wide as a split fence post.

Mharie stiffens beside me. "Bastard."

I park the truck, and before I can stop her, she's out the door, boots crunching on frost. She cuts a line through the crowd straight toward Wendell, shoulders squared like a general going to war.

"Hell." I scramble after her, weaving through strollers and lawn chairs.

By the time I reach her, she's already nose to nose with him. "Ye think scrawling on a barn makes ye a man?" she spits. Her voice carries, heads turning. "Ye'll nae break what Henry built, nor what I'll defend."

Wendell chuckles, loud enough for the crowd. "Fiery, aren't you? Must be that Highland blood." He tips his chin toward me, lazy and mean. "Still hanging on the arm of that city boy playing cowboy. Henry'd roll in his grave."

Gasps ripple through the crowd. Mharie surges forward, her fists curled. She looks ready to plant one square on his smug jaw. I catch her around the waist and haul her back, her boots skidding in the frost. "Not here," I grind out low in her ear, holding tight while she thrashes once. She's strong, small but all fire, and it takes everything I have to keep her tucked against me.

The crowd eats it up. Some shocked gasps, some titters of laughter, even a low whistle from somewhere near the bandstand. Wendell just grins wider, feeding on it.

"See there," he calls, voice oily. "She's wild, just like I said. Piper Falls doesn't need wild. It needs steady."

I step forward, keeping Mharie tucked firmly to my side. "Paint washes off. Lies don't. Careful what you try to spread, Wendell."

For the first time, his smirk flickers. Just a crack. Enough.

"Patrick. Mharie."

The voice comes from the courthouse steps. Mick, Henry's solicitor, stands there with his leather satchel and a wool scarf pulled tight against the wind. He waves us over, brows drawn.

We leave Wendell behind, though I feel his eyes drilling holes into our backs, and meet Mick at the steps.

"I was hoping to catch you both today," he says, lowering his voice.

"I'll want you in my office as soon as possible morning. We'll prepare affidavits, go over Henry's will again, and gather anything that proves the stability of residency. The vandalism," he pauses, eyes flicking between us, "could be useful, but only if you can tie it directly to Wendell. Otherwise, it muddies waters."

Beside me, Mharie's fingers twitch. She wants to mention the trail cameras, I can feel it. But I tighten my grip on her arm, answering for us both. "We'll be there."

Mick nods, already moving back toward the steps. "Stay visible today. Let the town see you together. It matters more than you think."

The band strikes up then, brass sharp against the cold air. The parade's about to roll, and the crowd surges toward the street, leaving us in a little bubble of quiet at the base of the courthouse.

Mharie looks up at me, fire still blazing in her eyes, but her voice cracks softer. "Right after Christmas. I thought..." She shakes her head, a humorless laugh. "It just hit me that this may be my last Christmas at Henry's house."

I brush a strand of hair from her cheek. "Then we'll make it the best damn Christmas Piper Falls ever saw."

And then the parade swallows us. Floats creak past, hay bales stacked high and kids waving paper snowflakes. The high school band blares "Jingle Bells," horns sharp enough to rattle teeth. I keep my arm firm around Mharie's shoulders, thumb stroking slow circles through her coat sleeve. Every so often, I catch Wendell's eyes across the way, smug and waiting, and I tighten my grip, make sure the town sees her pressed close against me.

"They're staring," she mutters under her breath.

"Good," I murmur back, brushing a kiss against the crown of her braid. "Let 'em."

Sure enough, whispers ripple around us. Mrs. Bailey nudges her friend, whispering behind a gloved hand. A gaggle of teenagers snicker, and one of the Walker boys hollers, "Go on, Patrick!" like it's all sport.

Mharie flushes, still fuming, but her shoulders ease under my touch. Slowly, like a kettle coming off the boil. She leans against me at last, whether she means to or not. I rest my chin on the top of her head, eyes forward on the parade, letting everyone see it plain. Wendell can grin all he wants. The only show he's getting is this: me and Mharie, standing together, steady as stone.

And in my gut, I know it. I won't let her lose that land. Not to Wendell. Not ever.

But the minute we're back at Henry's place and the truck's barely stopped rolling, Mharie's fury—the one she held down through the whole parade—detonates. She's out of the cab before I cut the engine. And I know before I even reach the porch: She is going to break.

And I'm going to be the one to catch her.

Chapter Twenty-Two

Mharie

I make it three steps inside before everything in me snaps loose. The door slams behind me, rattling the glass, and I don't even care if the house shakes down around us. My chest heaves like I've run a mile, my heart hammers like I have nothing in my veins but adrenaline and rage, every muscle hums with fury that refuses to listen to reason. My boots clatter across the floorboards as I pace the narrow strip between the table and the counter, fists clenched, muttering under my breath words so sharp they could cut glass.

The wool skirt swishes against my legs, itchy and unfamiliar. I'd only put it on because the parade felt like it called for Sunday best, and now I wish I'd worn trousers I could stomp around in properly. Patrick doesn't move. He just hangs his hat on the peg and leans against the door, arms crossed like he's watching a storm roll in. His calm only makes me burn hotter.

"Ye should've let me claw his eyes oot!" I whirl on him, voice too loud in the small space. My hands are fists at my sides, itching to swing.

Patrick's voice comes low, steady as a rock. "That's exactly what he wanted, Mharie. You gave him plenty already. Don't hand him the rest of you too."

I shove at his chest, hard enough that his back thumps the door. "Dinnae tell me what he wants. I've kenned Wendell Sutton most of my life, and he "

Patrick catches my wrists before I can strike again. His grip is firm but not cruel, his thumbs stroking the frantic beat of my pulse. He tilts his head down, those dark eyes fixed on me.

"I admire it," he murmurs.

I blink. "Admire what?"

"Your fire. The way you'll tear the world apart for what's yours." His mouth twitches like he almost smiles. "Scares the hell out of me. And turns me on more than I should admit."

Heat slams through me faster than the fury. The room tilts, not from rage but from the way his words coil low in my belly. I lunge before I can think, smashing my mouth against his. The kiss is not sweet. Its teeth and heat and a growl torn from the back of my throat. Patrick answers in kind, one hand sliding into my hair, tugging my head back so he can deepen it. His other arm circles my waist, hauling me against the solid wall of his body.

I bite his lip. He groans, the sound vibrating straight through me, and then we're stumbling together, half-blind, half-drunk on want.

We hit the counter, dishes rattling. Patrick lifts me with maddening ease, setting me atop the wooden surface, his hips pressing between my knees. My skirt tangles and bunches, fabric sliding high as my legs wrap around him. I'd worn it for the town, but here in our kitchen, it's nothing but a nuisance.

"You drive me mad," I hiss against his mouth.

"Good." His breath is hot on my skin as he drags kisses down my neck. "Because you're driving me insane."

I clutch at his shoulders, nails digging through the fabric, desperate to get closer. The air smells of sawdust and smoke clinging to him, the taste of coffee still on his tongue. Every sense is filled with Patrick. The world shrinks to the scrape of his stubble on my throat, the rough grip of his hands at my waist, the maddening way he pulls back just enough to make me chase him.

"I want " My voice breaks on a gasp as he nips at my collarbone.

"I know." He looks up at me, pupils blown wide, chest heaving. "I've wanted you since the moment you stood in that barn and called me a bloody fool."

A laugh bubbles out of me, wild and breathless. "Ye are a bloody fool."

"Then let me be your fool." His mouth claims mine again, softer now, but no less desperate.

He huffs a laugh, pressing a kiss into my hair. "The feeling's mutual."

Time blurs. The fury that sent me pacing melts into fire of another kind, leaving me weak and trembling in his arms. When we finally collapse together onto the couch, tangled in each other, I can barely breathe for the weight of it of him, of us. His hand slides under my blouse, rough and calloused, tracing the line of my spine. I arch into his touch, a soft moan escaping my lips. Patrick slowly begins to unbutton my blouse, his fingers deft and sure. I nearly beg him to just rip it off, but I stop myself. The cool air of the house hits my skin, and my nipples harden with the cold. He leans down, capturing one peak in his mouth, warming it, his tongue swirling around the sensitive flesh. I gasp, my hands tangling in his hair, urging him on.

Patrick's hands roam my body, memorizing every curve and dip, unhooking my bra with a flick of his wrist before tossing it to the floor. His stubble roughs against my soft skin as his mouth trails down my stomach. I squirm in anticipation, my body aching with need. He hooks his fingers in the waistband of my skirt, pulling it down slowly, his eyes never leaving mine. I lift my hips, helping him slide it off, leaving me in nothing but my underwear.

"You're so beautiful," he murmurs, his voice husky with desire. He runs a hand up my thigh, his touch sending shivers down my spine. I spread my legs, inviting him closer, my breath coming in ragged gasps. He leans down, his breath hot on my inner thigh, and I tremble with anticipation. His tongue flicks out, tracing a path up my thigh, and I moan, my hips bucking off the couch.

Patrick takes his time, teasing and tasting, hands roaming my body. I writhe beneath him, my body on fire, desperate for release. He slides a finger inside me, curving it to hit that sweet spot, and I cry out, my body clenching around him. He adds another finger, pumping in and out, his thumb circling my clit. I grind against his hand, chasing my orgasm, my body trembling with need.

"Patrick," I gasp, my voice broken. "Please."

He looks up at me, his eyes dark with desire, and smiles. "Not yet, my spitfire." He continues his torment, his fingers and tongue driving me wild. I claw at the couch, my body shaking with the effort of holding back. Finally, he takes mercy on me, his fingers moving faster, his thumb pressing down on my clit. I explode, my body convulsing with pleasure, waves of ecstasy washing over me. I cry out his name, my body milking his fingers, my orgasm going on and on.

Patrick crawls up my body, his eyes never leaving mine. He kisses me deeply, his tongue exploring my mouth, and I taste myself on him. I reach for his belt, my hands shaking with anticipation. He helps me, and soon, he's naked and poised at my entrance. I wrap my legs around his waist, urging him on, and he slides into me with one smooth thrust.

We both moan, our bodies fitting together perfectly. He starts to move, his hips rolling against mine, his pace fast and hard. I meet him thrust for thrust, my body clenching around him, my nails digging deep into his back. He picks up the pace, his hips slamming into mine, his breath coming in ragged gasps. I wrap my legs tighter around him, urging him deeper, harder, faster.

"Patrick " His name rips out of me on a gasp, my body trembling, every nerve strung tight. "Christ, I'm near again... I cannae hold it."

He leans down, capturing my mouth in a fierce kiss, his tongue mimicking the movements of his hips. I moan into his mouth, my body trembling with need. He reaches between us, fingers finding my clit, and I explode again, my body convulsing around him; my orgasm ripping through me like a tidal wave of fire. He follows me over the edge, his body shaking with the force of his release, my name a whispered prayer on his lips.

We collapse together, our bodies slick with sweat, our breaths coming in ragged gasps. Patrick rolls to the side as much as he can on the couch, pulling me tight against him, his arm wrapped around my waist. I rest my head on his chest, his heart beating a soothing pulse under my ear. His hand strokes down my spine, soothing where I hadn't known I ached.

"You scare me, you know that?" I whisper.

He huffs a laugh, pressing a kiss into my hair. "The feeling's mutual."

Silence stretches, warm and heavy. My anger's gone, replaced with something fiercer still: the knowledge that in his arms, I'm not alone in this fight.

"He doesn't win as long as we're standing like this," Patrick says at last, voice thick with conviction.

My throat tightens. I don't answer, because the truth is lodged too deep to speak aloud that Wendell Sutton can spray his poison on every barn in Texas, but he'll never touch what I've just found here.

I close my eyes, letting his warmth seep into me, and for the first time since Henry's death, I drift toward sleep without fear gnawing at my chest.

Chapter Twenty-Three

Patrick

Morning settles easily over the kitchen, like the house decided to keep one hand on last night's warmth. Mharie's at the table with sleeves pushed high and flour to her elbows, hair in a knot that's losing the battle. She has an old recipe card propped up in a teacup. The edges are soft, the ink pale with age. She reads it like a letter from somebody she misses.

"What's on the schedule?" I ask, filling the kettle even though she's clearly winning breakfast without me.

"Clootie dumplin'," she says, a little reverent and a little mischievous. "Ye cannae have Christmas without it. Fruit and spice tied in cloth, boiled till it sets and tastes like memory."

"Boiled dessert," I say, leaning on the counter. "New York will need a minute."

"New York can take a seat," she says, lips twitching. "This one's for Walker Ranch tomorrow. A bit o' home for their table." Her voice softens at *home*. She tips chopped apples and raisins into the bowl, and the kitchen smells like December. You can eat it with a spoon. My phone buzzes against the counter, flashing Brandon's name. I step aside and take the call.

"Morning," he says. "I read your text. Barn got tagged. You need to tighten things up before Sutton tries a second act."

"We started already," I tell him. "Trail cams have been up. We need more, though, if we want to put him in his place."

"Good start," he says, gears already turning. "Add floodlights on the corners, motion-activated with narrow cones. Put the fixtures high, out of reach. Crossbar on the big barn doors. Driveway gravel so you can hear tires at night. And I'll ship two cell-enabled cams for the road approach. If they cut Wi-Fi, you still get pings."

"Copy." I jot notes with a carpenter's pencil on the back of an envelope. "You want me to set a tripwire and dig a pit next?"

"That's phase two," he deadpans, then softens. "You sure you don't want me down there? Adam's pacing holes in my floor, swears he'll rent a plane."

"I've got it," I say, and mean it. "But keep the box coming."

He exhales. "Alright. One more thing talk to neighbors. Get eyes on each other's places. Community watch, ranch edition."

"Already on my list."

"Good man. Oh, and tilt the cams down enough to get a clear view of the faces. I'm not flying across the country to ID Wendell by his hat brim."

"Noted." I glance over to see Mharie watching me over the bowl, amused like she heard every word.

"Hardening the homestead?" she asks.

"Locks and light," I say.

She slides the bowl toward me and nods at the spoon. "Taste. Tell me if it needs more."

I dip a corner of the spoon, taste. Dark sugar. Orange. Warm spice. A little heat from soaked raisins. "Not bad," I admit, surprised. "Better than I expected."

Her smile tilts, proud and quiet. "Mum always said it tastes like the house remembers. Every Hogmanay, she'd say it like a prayer."

I reach to set the spoon down and catch a crescent of flour on her cheekbone. "You've got "

"Leave it," she says, eyes bright. "Proof I'm working."

I leave the flour and kiss her anyway, because I can. Coffee and clove, and a slight sound she only ever makes for me. When I pull back, she looks steadier somehow. So do I.

"String," she says briskly, clearing her throat. "And the cloth. We'll tie him snug."

Mharie flours an old tea towel; I hold the corners as instructed while she lowers the heavy dough into the center and cinches it like a parcel. The pot takes it with a hush, and soon steam unfurls through the kitchen and the whole house shifts a half inch closer to Christmas.

By midmorning, the air's sharp and clean and the sun is promising another sunny day filled with nothing but blue skies. Frost crunches under our boots as we cross to the barn. The floodlight boxes are stacked on the porch like sentries waiting to be sworn in. I shoulder one and climb the ladder while she braces her feet and scolds me when I lean too far.

"Mark me a line," I say.

She stretches up with a pencil, the tip dragging crisp graphite against the wood. Her elbow knocks my thigh, and everything goes momentarily quiet and warm. We both pretend it doesn't.

"Hold," she says, foreman-serious.

"Yes, ma'am," I answer, because it makes her roll her eyes.

The drill bites and the bracket seats, and every turn of the screw feels like staking a claim. We move along the gable. She feeds wire. I clip and staple. The floodlights take their places high, bright, out of reach eyes that will cut the yard wide open at night.

"Henry holds ladders like this?" I ask.

"Aye." She squints up at me. "Told me no further than three rungs. First chance I got, I went tae the fourth to spite him."

"Rebel."

"Ye've nae idea."

I do actually. I've watched her plant both feet in the middle of Main Street and refuse to be small.

We mount more trail cams on cedar posts at the east and west breaks, angle them down to catch faces. She teases me for fussing, calls me particular. I call her my supervisor, and she pretends not to like it. I set a driveway bell at the gate old pie tins wired above a fresh strip of rock. Step wrong and the whole place will sound like a junkyard Christmas.

"Ye'll nae overdo it?" she says as I heft the four-by-four crossbar and settle it into steel brackets across the big barn doors.

"If there's a fence to mend, I mend it. A lock to set, I set it." I lean my shoulder against the timber and feel its weight settle home. "If there's a light to flip on when a man with bad intentions steps wrong, I want that light flipping."

Her gaze lingers on me longer than the hardware. " Ye kept me from givin' him any more of what he wanted yesterday. "

"I'll keep doing it," I say, meeting her eyes. "Every time you need."

Something in her eases. The kind of breath people forget they're holding.

Which is when Dougal, feeling left out of the crew, shoves his nose into my open toolbox and lifts his head with a roll of electrical tape stuck to his lip. He blinks, cross-eyed, betrayed by physics.

"You absolute eejit," she laughs, rubbing between his eyes while I rescue the tape. He leans into her like a dog, a two-thousand-pound argument for staying.

By noon, the frost is gone, and mud streaks our boots. Floodlights squat clean under the eaves. Security cameras blink their tiny LEDs the only evidence of our upgrades. An iron crossbar sits patiently, leaned against the wall, waiting to brace a door.

Back inside, the kitchen is warm and damp and sweet. We haul the dumpling from the pot and set it to steam on a rack by the stove. When she peels the cloth back, the pudding holds, bronzed, dimpled, handsome in a way that has nothing to do with pretty.

We let it sit by the range while we clean the counter and wash the dishes. At the table, she brings out a battered tin of crayons and a stack of slips. "Wishes," she says. "We'll hang them tomorrow. One for us, a few we'll help grant."

She writes the first slow: *That we keep Henry's land.* Below it, smaller: *That I earn it.*

"You do," I say, simple as a fencepost. "Every day."

Her mouth presses a line, eyes bright.

She writes one more and hides it with her hand. I glance away, but not before I catch the first three words: *For Patrick to...* She tucks it under the tin before I can read more. I pretend I didn't see. The truth of it hums between us anyway.

"Brandon's shipping the cell cams," I say, sliding my phone aside. "Until then, I'll rig dummy housings by the road to spook anyone casing the place. Paint numbers on the gates, set reflective tacks on the fence breaks. If we ever need to call anything in, we'll have exact points."

"Ye planning tae sleep between now and Hogmanay?" she asks, no sting, just fond.

"I will," I say, "when the floodlights wake a Sutton at the worst possible moment."

"There's a thought tae warm a Scot," she says, cheeks dimpling.

We tag the dumpling with *Campbell Homestead* in her neat hand and a tiny thistle doodle on the corner. She tucks the wish slips into an envelope and ties it with red twine. Simple things. All of them are heavier than they look.

"Tomorrow," she says, looking in the direction of Walker Ranch, "folk will hang their wishes."

I lace my fingers through hers. "We'll hang one of ours."

Her hand tightens. "Aye. That we keep what's Henry's."

We stand in that quiet together until the light gleans. I jog to the breaker and flip the switch. The yard floods white as a stadium on a stormy night. Shadows scuttle back under the fence rails and hide. The barn glows. Even the cedar stump looks guilty.

"That'll make a man think twice," she says, low.

"Good," I say. "Let him."

She leans into me, and I wrap an arm around her shoulders, my knuckles brushing the braid down her back. Our meeting with Mick sits on the calendar. A court date is set for just after Christmas. But right now, under our own bright making, with a pudding cooling by the stove and wishes folded neat in a tin, I can say *ours* out loud and not feel like I'm lying to the dark.

Chapter Twenty-Four

Mharie

The Walker Ranch shines brighter than I've ever seen it. Electric lanterns bob from the trees, strung on tinsel that catches every bit of frost until the whole place glitters. A big blue spruce stands tall at the center, showcasing sparkling ornaments, multiple bows, and wrapped in ribbon, its evergreen branches hung heavy with slips of paper that flutter like prayers. Cars line the road, boots crunch over gravel, and laughter spills into the cold.

Patrick pulls us into a space beside a line of pickups and cuts the engine.

"Ready?"

I smooth the front of my coat, though it does little for the nerves simmering under my ribs. "That's a question with only one wrong answer."

He grins, quick and crooked. "Then give me the right one."

"Fine," I mutter, rolling my eyes. "Aye, I'm ready."

He knows better than to press.

I cradle the clootie dumpling against my chest, bundled in tartan, still carrying the faint spice-sweet warmth it held yesterday. It smells like cinnamon, treacle, and spice like the kitchens of my childhood, though I've never admitted that to anyone here. Patrick pushes the door open for me, and folk step aside as we pass, nodding, smiling. A Whitaker lad tips his hat. One of the women from Lone Star Feed waves us toward the barn, calling, "Glad you came, Mharie!"

I almost stumble at that. *Glad you came.* As if I belong here.

Inside the big barn, tables sag beneath casseroles, pies, and trays of roasted meats. Crockpots line the back wall, steam curling into the rafters. Kids dart between legs, slips of paper clutched in mittened fists. Everywhere I look, it's color and bustle and noise, the kind of gathering Henry used to talk about with a fondness I never quite believed.

We carry the dumpling to the end of the dessert table, and I set it down with more care than I mean to. A couple of women hover nearby, peering curiously.

"What's this one?" one asks, nudging the tartan bundle.

I smooth the cloth open, showing the bronzed, dimpled surface. "Clootie dumplin'," I say, gentler than I expected. "Ye cannae have Hogmanay without it. It's fruit and spice, boiled in cloth till it sets. My mum always said it tastes like the house remembers."

Their eyes widen, and one of the women lets out a low whistle. "Boiled dessert?"

I laugh, not sharply but easily. "Aye. Strange tae you maybe, but it holds well. Slice it like cake, serve it warm or cold. There's plenty o' spice in there cinnamon, nutmeg, treacle."

"Smells incredible," another says, leaning closer. "Henry would've loved that you're here."

My throat tightens, but I nod. "Aye."

They smile, not with pity, but with pleasure, and move on. I'm left standing at the table with the tartan cloth bunched in my hands, my heart a little lighter. The steam from the crockpots curls in the rafters, sweet and savory scents tangling until the whole barn feels warm enough to melt the frost from my bones.

Patrick's hand brushes the small of my back, steering me gently through the press of neighbors toward the great spruce in the center. Ribbons catch the lantern light overhead, fluttering like sparks. Children dart past with slips clutched tight, laughter trailing behind them.

It doesn't take long to notice the duplicates. Two of the same wish flutter past me on different branches: *I wish for a baby brother. I wish for a baby brother.* For a moment, I thought the child was just ambitious.

A mother near the cider table explains, "Each child wrote two slips one for the church basket, so we adults can grant them, and one for the tree." She laughs, tucking her scarf tighter. "Saves tears when the branches come down."

Another chimes in, "Besides, the tree's for the stars to see. You don't want to cheat them of their chance, do you?"

As if to prove the point, a boy barrels past me, boots clumsy, ribbon clenched in his fist. "This one's for the tree so the sky knows!" he hollers, tying it to a low branch with a flourish. The crowd cheers him like he's just roped a bull.

Something stings the back of my throat. Without thinking, I move closer to Patrick, my hand slipping through the crook of his arm. Solid, steady. He doesn't comment, just shifts enough to make space for me.

We weave toward the spruce, stopping when a little girl with braids tugs my coat.

"Can you tie mine? Papa says I'm too small."

Her slip says *I wish for a baby brother.* I nearly laugh, nearly cry. "Let's put it where the stars can see it best," I tell her. I knot it low enough for her to reach, and she beams up at me with a gap-toothed grin.

"Thank you!" Then she's gone, swallowed by cousins.

Patrick's watching, something soft in his gaze. My cheeks heat, and I busy myself straightening ribbons that don't need it.

More slips flutter past my hands. One scrawled in block letters: *Fourteen glitter pens, please and thank you.* I can't help but grin; I take it from the branch, envisioning the biggest batch of glitter pens I can find. Another: *For my granddad's radio to work again.* That one I pass to Patrick without thinking. He tucks it in his coat pocket, murmuring, "I'll see what I can do." And I believe him.

While I linger with the slips, Patrick drifts toward a cluster of men near the cider barrels ranchers, Whitakers, and a couple from Lone Star Feed. I half expect him to stand apart, New York written all over him, but he doesn't. He listens, asks after calving, and nods when they grumble about the early frost. One claps his shoulder, another chuckles at something he says. Patrick's stance is easy, shoulders loose, like he's been here all along.

The sight roots me more than anything else tonight. He isn't just standing with me. He's standing with *them.*

The lanterns are lit as the crowd gathers close. The spruce glows gold, paper slips catching the light until they shimmer like constellations caught in branches. Children stomp and clap, their boots thudding out a rhythm before a carol rises, ragged but strong.

A hush comes first, like the whole barn holds its breath. Then voices climb, rough but true, and the sound rolls warm through the rafters. Breath clouds in the cold, lantern glass fogging. For once, I don't feel outside looking in I'm inside, part of the noise and the song.

Patrick's arm curves warm around my shoulders, pulling me in so the wind cuts less.

"They're staring," I mutter.

"Good," he whispers against my hair. "Let them."

I do. I let the whole town see me pressed against him, his thumb stroking slow circles on my sleeve. Whispers ripple but it isn't cruel. It's teasing, fond, the kind of ribbing you only get when folk count you as their own.

Eyes meet mine across the glow of the lanterns, and instead of suspicion and gossip, I find nods, smiles, mugs raised in quiet cheer. Martha from Lone Star Feed mouths *about time*. Dale winks, tipping his hat. For the first time since I set foot back in Piper Falls, it feels less like I'm being watched and more like I'm being welcomed.

Slowly, like a kettle taken off the boil, my shoulders ease. My anger at Wendell, my fear of losing Henry's place none of it stands a chance under the quiet truth settling in my chest: no one here ever pushed me out. I was the one holding myself apart, convinced I didn't belong.

A boy too small for his boots toddles past with a ribbon, trips, and I instinctively bend to help him up, patting frost from his knees. He beams at me, clutching his slip. "It's for my dog," he whispers, as if it's a secret. "So he comes home."

My throat closes. "Then let's put it high, so the stars can find it quicker." We tie the ribbon together, mittened hands clumsy but determined, and the boy runs off.

I rise, wiping my hands on my coat, and Patrick's already watching me still, quiet, something warm flickering in his eyes. And when his hand lifts, just barely, an invitation instead of an assumption... mine moves toward his like it was always meant to.

Not the act. Not the show. Just us.

And in that moment, under the glow of lanterns and the weight of a hundred paper wishes, I know I belong here. To Henry's land. To Piper Falls. To Patrick, whether I meant to or not.

Chapter Twenty-Five

Patrick

The house feels different this morning.

Not new, not changed in its bones, but lighter somehow. The floors still creak in the same places, the stove still rattles when it warms, and Dougal still bellows if breakfast doesn't come fast enough. But after last night at Walker Ranch, the air in here carries something softer. Like the place remembered it was meant to be lived in. Mharie hums under her breath as she rinses mugs at the sink, her hair twisted up in some careless knot. No defenses, no sharp edge. Just... herself. That's rarer than she knows. I sit at the kitchen table with my hands wrapped around a mug of coffee, watching steam curl. Across the yard, the barn door still hangs too loosely on its hinges, scarred with Wendell's red spray paint that makes my blood boil. We scrubbed most of it off, but the ghost of those letters lingers if you know where to look.

I'd promised her we'd make it secure, and I meant it.

My phone buzzes on the table. Brandon again this time with "phase two" suggestions. Once the basics are in, add tamper plates to the camera posts. And strip the screws so they can't be backed out. A follow-up: Also put reflective tacks on the fence breaks. Gives a cleaner grid if you ever need to track footprints. I text back: On it. Quit micromanaging. He responds with a thumbs-up emoji and a middle finger. When I glance up, Mharie's leaning against the counter with a tartan dish towel in her hands, watching me.

"Is that your brother?"

"Yeah. Making sure I don't slack off."

Her lips twitch. "Good. Saves me the bother."

I bark out a laugh and shake my head. "Once the cell cams land, I'll set them before dark. Thinking about adding a motion alarm inside the barn. Quiet but enough to wake us if he slips in. "

She nods, arms crossed, but not in that shut-me-out way. "We'll get them up quick."

"We?"

"Aye, we. Ye didn't think I'd leave it tae you alone, did ye?" Her brows lift, daring me to argue.

I don't. Because the truth is, the sound of her saying *we* does more to steady me than anything else.

By midmorning, I head into Piper Falls for hardware. Mharie rides along, sitting quietly with her gaze fixed on the passing fields. At the counter, folks greet me differently than they used to. Not wary. Not sizing me up just familiar, like I passed some test I didn't know I was taking. "Williams," the clerk says with a nod, ringing up the hinges. "Saw you at Walker Ranch last night. Good to see you pitching in."

A man by the door adds, "You and Mharie looked right at home. Henry'd be glad for that." It throws me a little not because I'm used to indifference, but because Willow Glen was the same way. Small towns talk, notice everything, hold tight to their own. I just didn't expect Piper Falls to fold me in so quickly. Beside me, Mharie stiffens at first ready to argue, ready to defend but when the shopkeeper smiles at her, saying, "That dumpling you brought was something else," her posture softens. She thanks him, cheeks coloring faintly, and I swear it's the first time I've seen her *accept* a compliment from this town instead of batting it away.

Back home, we unload the hardware onto the porch. I'm halfway through testing one of the new hinges when I hear her phone buzz from inside. Her footsteps cross the floor, quick, then pause. She answers, voice shifting sharper, clearer. Her accent digs in like it always does when Scotland calls.

I catch fragments through the open window. Aye, that time-line still works. … I'll be back before Hogmanay. … Thank ye for the chance.

My grip tightens on the screwdriver. The words aren't for me, but they hit anyway, back *before Hogmanay.* That's New Year's. Which means she's planning to go.

When she comes out a few minutes later, she doesn't meet my eyes right away. "Professor," she says lightly, tucking her phone into her pocket. "Wanted tae confirm a few things for the new year."

I nod, keeping my tone even. "Good news, then."

"Aye." Her answer is clipped, her hands fidget with the edge of her sweater.

I don't press. But the knot in my chest says maybe I should.

By afternoon, I'm outside again, tightening the porch gate with a new crossbar. The hinge still shrieks when it swings, which is perfect. If Wendell ever tries to slip through at night, I want the whole place to hear him coming.

Mharie putters inside, fussing over jars and tins. Every so often, she calls out a Gaelic phrase I can't make sense of, and I answer with a grunt. It feels domestic, comfortable like we've done this a hundred times before.

Dougal wanders too close, knocking the hammer clean out of my hand with one swinging horn. I curse, and from the window I hear her laugh, rich and unguarded. "Don't encourage him," I growl, retrieving the hammer from the dirt.

She leans out the window, eyes sparkling. "Och, he likes tae help. Ye should be grateful."

"Next time, he can split the wood."

Her laugh carries, light and musical, and I can't help the grin tugging at my mouth. By dusk, the day winds down. The chores are done, the barn's secured, the new hinge holds steady. We eat stew and bread, quiet except for the crackle of the stove. Later we move into the living room with mugs of cocoa, lamplight soft and the fire burning low. Dougal bellows from the pasture, but inside it's warm, cocooned. I watch her curl into the armchair across from me, tartan throw draped over her lap. For once, she looks at ease no sharpness in her shoulders, no fight in her eyes. Just tired, and maybe a little wistful.

I clear my throat. "That call earlier. Scotland?"

Her gaze lifts, cautious. "Aye. My professor. The placement's still waiting. They expect me."

"And you want to go?"

She stares into her mug, cocoa swirling dark. "It's what I worked for. What I thought I wanted." Her voice falters, softer. "But now..." Silence stretches. She doesn't finish the thought, but she doesn't have to. Her eyes flick around the room the fire, the worn rug, the curtains she'd tied back earlier, finally to me.

I lean forward, resting my forearms on my knees. "Whatever choice you make... I just want it to be yours. Not forced by Wendell. Not by me."

Her lips part like she wants to argue, but instead she swallows and nods, small and sure. We sit in the quiet for a long time, the fire crackling between us. Then, almost without thinking, she shifts to the couch beside me, her knee brushing mine. I cover her hand with mine, solid and steady. No promises. No grand declarations. Just that small weight, anchoring us both.

For the first time since all this started, it feels like we're not just holding the line we're building something that can last.

Chapter Twenty-Six

Mharie

The morning of Christmas Eve, I wake to a quiet that doesn't belong to Texas.

The kind that makes you hold your breath in case you scare it away. When I lift the curtain, the yard is dusted white just a skiff, nothing a Highland winter would brag about but enough to turn the pasture into a held-breath miracle. The porch rail wears a thin sugar edge. The fence lines glow pale. For a heartbeat, I swear I can hear Henry laughing in my ear, "Well, now, look at that."

"Patrick," I whisper, shaking his shoulder. "Snow."

He's up fast, all wary instinct, until he sees outside. Then he grins soft, like the kind that's only for me. "Merry Christmas, Texas style."

We pull on coats and boots over pajamas and step into the cold. Air nips the insides of my nostrils. Somewhere out by the pines, Dougal bellows with theatrical importance, and then the big daft beast comes trotting, head low, whiskers coated with frost.

He paws the ground, tosses a little clump of white into the air, then prances after it as if it's alive. I laugh so hard I have to grab the porch post.

"Aye, show off," I call. "Go on then."

The coos are at it too, shaggy backs pillowed with powder, kicking up their heels like calves. It's ridiculous and pure, and it jabs something soft and aching inside me. This place choosing joy without asking permission.

Patrick steals a look at me instead of the herd, hands sunk in coat pockets. "They handle it better than most Texans."

"Better than you?" I challenge.

"Not a chance." He nudges my shoulder with his. "I'm from New York. We're born grumpy at snow."

We feed early, breath steaming as we pitch hay. The light grows in slow layers, and by the time we've checked the trough heaters and peeked at the trail-cam indicator lights, my fingers are stinging and my nose is numb. We head inside with that good farm-morning ache in our bones.

While the kettle sings, Patrick sets the little tin of short-bread I baked on the table and steals two pieces before the tea's poured. I swat his hand, but my heart isn't in it.

"The meeting with Mick is coming up," I say, because peace never lasts long when worry's waiting its turn.

He nods, serious again. "We'll be ready."

We turn the living room into a war room. The coffee table disappears beneath neat stacks: the will, Henry's tax receipts, feed invoices, the letter from Lone Star Feed about our account being current, printouts from the trail-cam portal with timestamps, phone photos of the red slur stamped across the barn. I write titles on sticky notes in my tidy student hand. Patrick hole-punches and slides everything into a binder he labeled HIGHLAND HOMESTEAD EVIDENCE. It looks ordinary. It feels like armor.

"Affidavits," he says, tapping the list. "Mick will draft them, but we should prep names. Folks who can speak to you running the place. Stability of residency, all that. We need to get all this to him the day after Christmas so it can be prepared before court on the twenty ninth."

"Dale from the feed. Mrs. Ortiz she's seen me fix the fence by the road almost every week. And the Whitaker lad's father helped me with a calf pull the week I arrived."

"Good," he says, and writes them in block letters, clean and quick. "Photos of you working "

"I'll nae stick a camera on my head," I mutter, but I dig out my phone anyway. There I am, right after I arrived, covered to the elbows in iodine, grinning like a lunatic at a healthy calf. There I am again, muddy to the thighs, glaring at a broken gate. I print them off and he tucks each image behind a tab.

When we break for more tea, he catches my hand as I pass and pulls me onto the couch beside him.

"Let's practice," he says gently. "Just a few questions. So you're not blindsided."

My shoulders go tight before I can help it. "Aye. Go on then."

"Ms. Campbell, are you currently employed in Texas?"

"Aye," I answer, chin up. "On my own land."

"Do you have evidence that you reside here full-time?"

I gesture to the piles. "Bills, receipts, neighbors' testimony. And my word."

His next question lands harder. "Do you intend to continue residing in Texas permanently?"

My mouth goes dry. Permanently. The word crawls under my ribs. I open my mouth, close it again. "I "

Patrick's eyes flick up, warning so soft I almost miss it.

"I intend," I force out, spine straight, "to see through what I started here."

He doesn't let me breathe before the next blow. "And if opposing counsel suggests your... arrangement with Mr. Williams is for convenience?"

Heat flares under my ribs. He lifts one eyebrow, warning, and I breathe.

"I'll say I dinnae invite that kind of insult into Henry's house. And that my choices romantic or legal dinnae change the facts. I came back, and I've done the work every day since. This place stands because I made sure it did."

"Good," he murmurs, pride warm in his eyes. "Keep that tone. Calm. You were born to argue the truth."

We work like that for another hour, questions and answers, my spine loosening each time I survive the worst-case version. At last he snaps the binder shut and drags the tartan throw over both our legs.

"Enough for today," he decides. "It's Christmas Eve."

We make cocoa the way Henry taught me, with a spoon of treacle and a whisper of salt. Outside, snow still glitters on fence rails that were brown yesterday. The radio crackles to life with carols that don't quite find the right key. It's perfect.

By noon, the sky has already given back most of its white, but Dougal carries his brag on his back and refuses to shake it off. We watch him from the porch while Patrick straddles the bench and tightens the lag screws on the porch-gate crossbar again, fine-tuning it until it shrieks just the way he likes. He grins, testing it again.

"Ye love that horrid sound," I accuse.

He shrugs, pleased. "Music. If someone sneaks through this gate in the night, it wakes half the county."

"Aye, including the coos."

"Perfect."

The afternoon slides by quietly as a hymn. We fix minor things that have nagged me since I first arrived: a split porch step, a sagging kitchen drawer, and the latch that never quite catches in the mudroom. Every repair clicks something back into place in me too. The house remembers how to be held.

I pull out a shoebox from under the bed and lay a few old photos on the table. Henry in his good hat. Me at sixteen, all elbows and midge bites, sitting on the fence like I own the world. My parents are on a damp Scottish beach, hair blown wild, holding me between them like a secret.

"Ye'll come back with me one day," I tell him quietly, surprising myself. "Just to see. It's cold and the wind will cut ye in half, and I'll still want tae drag you along every cliff path until your feet ache."

He smiles without taking his eyes off my father's face. "Name the day."

My throat goes tight. "I dinnae ken when. But... that I want ye there. That I ken."

He turns his palm up on the table. I set my hand in it, smaller on his, and the quiet between us turns golden.

Later, by the fire, we unwrap what little we have. He produced a pair of good leather gloves from somewhere in town lined, sturdy, meant for winter chores and I pretend to scold him for spoiling me while secretly flexing my fingers inside them, greedy for the way they fit. I give him Henry's spare headlamp, a fresh stack of index cards for his lists, and a plain pewter key fob I found at the antique store last week. He runs his thumb over the metal as if it's holy.

"Ye'll keep that as long as you keep the keys that go with it," I say, forcing lightness into my tone.

He tucks it into his pocket with a look I can't name.

When the fire burns down to a bed of orange, we step back onto the porch with two blankets and one mug between us. Frost has set in where the snow melted. The yard brightens under floodlights when he flips the switch. The barn, the gates, the driveway they all glow. The cameras blink their tiny comfort.

"Tomorrow," I say, "We'll take a plate to the Ortiz house. Drop by Dale's with the tins. Then back here to rest."

He nods. "And tonight?"

"Tonight," I answer, leaning into his side until our shoulders lock, "we breathe."

We listen to the quiet. To Dougal's contented snore from the paddock. To the distant tick of a cooling roof. To the sound the land makes when it's briefly, blessedly at peace.

He tips my chin with his knuckle so I'll meet his eyes, then kisses me slowly, nothing like the hungry, reckless kisses we've already survived together. This one is quiet. Steady. The kind that says I'm here without asking for anything more. When he pulls back, the floodlights pick up the faintest smile at the corner of his mouth, the kind I'll put in a drawer for later when the room is too quiet and the worry too loud.

"Come inside," he says softly. "It's freezing, spitfire."

"Aye," I say, and steal one more look at our bright yard. "But it's ours."

We close the door on the cold. The house receives us without a creak. Tomorrow will bring its errands and the next day its fight. For now, I set the binder on the mantel like a sentinel, curl under his arm, and let the rare Texas snow turn to water in the gutters while our fire holds.

Chapter Twenty-Seven

Patrick

I wake to a ribbon tickling my mouth. Soft. Teasing. The kind of whisper that drags a groan out of my chest before I'm even fully here. Then I open my eyes and she's above me knees bracketing my hips, hair down, one glossy red bow pinned close to her temple like sin dressed as Christmas.

"Merry Christmas," she says, voice gone silk. "I'm the present."

My hand shoots up, palming her thigh through my shirt she stole last night. It's barely buttoned. It's not going to survive. "You wrapped yourself and climbed on me?"

"Aye." She bends, mouth hovering a breath above mine. "You gonna open me, Williams, or stare like a numpty?"

I fist the hem of my shirt at her waist and rip. Buttons scatter like sleet on the floorboards. She laughs sharp and delighted then gasps when I drag the torn fabric out of my way and get both hands full of warm, naked Mharie.

"God, look at you," I rasp. "Bow in your hair, nothing but trouble everywhere else."

"Take it, then," she dares, rolling her hips to grind against me exactly where I'm already hard. "If you can."

"Oh, sweetheart." I grip her, thumb circling slow where she's slick and aching. Her head tips back, the bow shining in the thin winter light. "I can."

She's smug for a heartbeat, and then I push two fingers deep, and her smugness evaporates into a broken, hungry sound that hits me square in the spine. She clenches, shivers, braces her hands on my chest, and rocks like she means to wreck me.

"Use me," I tell her, roughly. "Ride my hand. Take what you want."

She does. Jesus, she does hips greedy, breath stuttering in her lungs when I lift my head and catch her lower lip between my teeth. Outside, the world is quiet and bright, that rare Texas chill clinging to the glass. In here, she's heat and focus and everything I didn't know how to ask for, grinding against my palm until she's swearing in Gaelic and I'm losing my mind.

"Patrick "

"I've got you." I slide my thumb higher, press just right, and she comes apart hard clutching, gasping, eyes blown wide as the bow wobbles in her hair. I keep her there, right at the top of it, and kiss her through the tremors until she melts against me boneless and cursing me like a prayer.

"Show-off," she mutters against my mouth, still shaking. "Ye insufferable man."

"Turn over," I say, voice wrecked. "Now."

Her eyes flare challenge and trust, my favorite mix. She slides off and onto her stomach, knees tucked under, ass up, cheek turned to watch me. I plant one knee between her thighs, snag the belt from my robe hanging off the bedpost, and slow my fist around myself to watch her pupils blow again.

"Hands," I say.

She offers them behind her back without a single quip. I take the thin red ribbon from the nightstand the one she used to tie the bow in her hair. It's satiny and ridiculous. I loop it around her wrists, not tight just enough tension to make her breathe differently.

"This okay?" I murmur, leaning to kiss the shell of her ear.

"Aye." Barely a whisper. "Please."

My control snaps like the buttons on my shirt. I press in slowly, sink all the way, and swear into her skin when she squeezes around me like she has no intention of letting me go. She groans deep, filthy and pushes back to take every inch, bow still shining in her hair like a crown.

"Mine," I tell her, hips snapping, hand braced at her waist. "Right now, you're mine."

"Yours," she breathes, wrecked and perfect. "Take it."

So I do. I set a rhythm that punishes us both, the bedframe complaining, the winter-bright morning turning thin and wild around the edges. She's noise and heat, trying to arch her bound hands higher, and I pull her up against my chest with a fist in the ribbon, kiss her throat, and fuck the air right out of her.

She tips, falling her second one hitting fast and hard, all muscle and broken Gaelic. I follow a breath later with a curse that sounds like her name, spill deep, and hold there, shaking, until the world comes back in pieces the bow scratching my jaw when she turns her head, the sound of our breathing, the faint bellow of Dougal like he's offended he missed the show.

We collapse sideways in a tangle, the ribbon lax around her wrists. I ease it off, kiss the soft lines it left, and rub warmth into her hands until her fingers curl and flex.

Her body is slick with sweat, her skin flushed and glowing. I trail my fingers down her spine, feeling her shiver beneath my touch. She arches into me, her breath hitching as I tease the curve of her ass. I grip her hips, pulling her closer, feeling the heat of her against my throbbing cock.

"Patrick," she gasps, her voice a mix of pleasure and desperation. "More."

I oblige, thrusting into her with a force that makes the bed creak. She meets my movements, her body moving in sync with mine. The room fills with the sounds of our flesh meeting, the scent of sex heavy in the air.

I reach around, finding her clit with my fingers, circling it in time with my thrusts. She cries out, her body tensing as I push her closer to the edge. I can feel her muscles clenching around me, her body begging for release.

"Come for me, Mharie," I growl, my voice low and commanding. "Let me feel you come all over my cock."

She does, her body convulsing as she comes undone. I follow her over the edge, my own release tearing through me with a force that leaves me breathless. We collapse together, bodies entwined, breaths mingling as we ride out the aftershocks.

As we lie there, spent and sated, I can't help but smile.

"You okay?" I ask.

"Aye." She smiles at the ceiling, smug again. "Merry Christmas to me."

I laugh, drop a kiss on the bow, then push hair off her temple with my thumb. "You put that on just to kill me?"

"To ruin ye," she corrects, eyes gleaming. "Did it work?"

"Spectacularly."

We lie there and let the morning settle around us. The window's a pale square of frost-lit quiet. The house smells like cedar and last night's fire, and she smells like sweat and shortbread and the kind of trouble I would cross states for twice.

"Court's day in just a few days," she says at last, voice small in a way she hates.

"Yeah." I tuck the blanket higher over her bare shoulder, kiss the spot under her ear where she's softest. "You're ready."

A beat. "What if I'm not?"

"Then I'll stand up beside you and make the whole damn room listen." I tip her face to mine. "We've got the binder. The cameras. The neighbors. The truth. Wendell can bluster all he wants he doesn't get this land."

Her throat works. She nods, but the worry's still there buried, stubborn. "Ask me again," she says, and I know exactly which question she means. The one that made her stumble yesterday.

"Do you intend to keep residing in Texas," I murmur, gently, "permanently?"

Her eyes flick away, then back. Brave. "I intend," she says, steadying herself, "to see through what I started here."

It's not yes. It's not no. It's honest. It's her.

"Good," I say, thumb stroking her jaw. "The judge doesn't need poetry. He needs facts." I kiss her once more, slow, because I can't not. "Besides. I can wait for the rest."

The words nearly jump the rails and turn into something heavier. I bite them back. Not today. Not when the world is this quiet and the bow is still tied in her hair.

She must hear the unsaid, because she softens and scoots closer until her knee hooks over my hip. "We need to take cookie tins to the Ortiz house," she says into my throat. "Dale too. Smile. Be seen. But I want to be back before dusk."

"We will." I picture the route, the people, the way the town watches and adds up what it thinks it knows. Let them. "I'll re-check the lower shed lock before we go."

"And the porch-gate shriek you love," she mutters, pretending annoyance, failing.

I grin against her forehead. "Music, spitfire."

She snorts, kisses my chest once, then sits up hair wild, bow somehow still holding on, my shirt hanging off one shoulder in ribbons until she lets it fall to the floor. "You're going to run out of shirts at this rate," she mutters.

"I'll buy ten more for you to steal," I say, dragging her back for one more kiss that turns into another, then another. "But you're keeping the bow."

"You're impossible."

"And you're devastating."

She slides off the bed, naked but for that stupid, perfect bow, and pads toward the bathroom. She tosses a look over her shoulder that says, "Don't move." I don't. I watch her. I memorize the line of her back, the slight, confident tilt of her chin, the vulnerability she doesn't know she shows me when she thinks I'm not looking. It does something dangerous in my chest.

Not yet. Court first. Then we'll see what she chooses.

Water runs. Pipes knock. I drag on sweats, gather the buttons off the floor, and find one in the corner by the nightstand that I tuck into my pocket like an idiot.

She returns in jeans and a chunky sweater I want to peel her out of, bow relocated to the top of her braid, like she's daring me to misbehave. I do, stealing a kiss in the doorway to hear her laugh, then smacking her ass because I can't help myself.

"Coffee," she orders, grinning. "Then tins. Then home."

"Yes, ma'am." While the kettle hums, I watch her count out shortbread into the holiday tins, the bow bobbing when she moves.

We step onto the porch into a morning so clean it almost hurts thin frost along the rail, sun pushing off the last of the snow. The yard is bright. The cameras blink their small, steady language. Somewhere out in the pasture, Dougal bellows like he's the king of Christmas.

Tomorrow is another fight.

Today, she wore a bow in my bed, let me ruin her, then pulled herself together and chose the work again. Today, we show this town what we already know.

This place stands. And I'll make damn sure it stays that way.

Chapter Twenty-Eight

Mharie

The hallway outside the courtroom smells of old varnish, bitter coffee, and nerves. I sit on the hard bench and make a job of breathing: slow in, slower out, like it's something you can practice until it sticks. Mick sits to my left, suit neat as a ledger, a yellow pencil balanced between two fingers. Patrick stands behind us like a wall someone built on purpose, his palm a quiet weight at my shoulder when the corridor hums too loud. It steadies me without softening me.

"Answer only what's asked," Mick murmurs. "No more."

"Aye." My voice doesn't shake. That will do.

The gallery inside is already filling: Mrs. Ortiz in her sensible coat; Dale from the feed with grease he can't scrub from his hands; the Whitakers with their fencepost faces. Seeing them settles something in me that isn't law or paper. It's land.

Wendell waits down the hall with his solicitor, the cologne-heavy one. New hat today, brim too clean to be honest. He wears that grin he keeps for church and cameras, practiced at looking wronged and brave about it.

The bailiff opens the door. "Campbell v. Sutton."

My name sounds like business, all the softness scraped away. We stand. Patrick's thumb presses once against my palm steady, aye and we go in.

The courtroom eats sound. The judge is an older man with a thin mouth and eyes tired at the edges. He nods to counsel, surveys the benches like he's counting weights, and sits like the chair is a duty rather than a comfort. I remind myself he's human, with mismatched socks and cold toast. It doesn't help. My chest tightens anyway.

Mick opens like he's setting a post: straight, simple, no waste. He says Henry's name like a fact you can lean on. He lays out the will and inventory, then stewardship as if it's a thing the law can hold: receipts, vet logs, feed invoices, the letter from Lone Star Feed showing the account is current. Photographs with timestamps. He gives dates, not speeches. He provides the court with a map you can follow without muddy boots.

Wendell's solicitor rises slowly, like a man stretching before a show. "Ms. Campbell, isn't it true you were not present in the county when Mr. Sutton passed? That you spent the last two years abroad?"

Behind me, Patrick breathes steadily, lending me air.

"It is," I say, even. "I wasn't here when Henry died. I came back because I promised I would. I've worked the homestead every day since."

The man smiles with his mouth, not his eyes. "And would you say your current residency is... convenient to your relationship with Mr. Williams?"

"It isn't an arrangement," I cut in, precise. "It's my life. I fatten calves. I fix gates. I pay the bills. You can call the work convenient if you like. It won't change the facts."

His brows flick, scent of blood in the water, and he presses on: residency technicalities, staged photos, whether a woman in love makes foolish choices. He lays little traps and waits to see if I'll step wrong.

I don't. I answer exactly what's asked. I hand the judge clean things: dates, names, paper, trail-cam clips.

When the clerk plays the footage, a murmur runs down the benches like a wire struck. There I am in a worn jacket, hair yanked back, swearing at a straggler. Knee-deep in mud at the south gate, jaw set against a latch that won't bite. Timestamps show the truth. No glamour. Just work. And in one frame, a shadow slips along the fence line at 2:13 a.m. the shape of him, broad shoulders and that hitch in the step, enough to ripple the benches but not enough for proof.

Wendell's solicitor shifts gears, trading teeth for honey. Tradition. Lineage. Family. He never says "blood is the law," but he hopes the judge thinks it. He paints me as a lass with feelings instead of footing, as if land should go to the one who smiles least at funerals.

"Is Mr. Williams a resident?" he asks at last. There's the meat the trap.

My back goes straight. I know that move. He wants to reduce me to a woman with a man before he lets me be a woman with land.

Patrick stands when Mick nods. No swagger. "On and off," he says. "I stayed to secure the property after vandalism. Installed cameras. Bought materials. Handled dawn chores. The feed account is under Ms. Campbell's name. She makes the calls."

He doesn't look at me long. Keeps public and private in their lanes. The gallery watches him like he's an answer to a question they don't know how to ask.

Cross-exam claws where it can't bite. "Did Mr. Sutton ever say he intended you to inherit the property?"

"Aye. Henry raised me since I was a young girl. He told me I was meant to care for it , and I gave him my word I would."

"But nothing in writing?"

"He did write it. It's called a will. Everything else he said to my face."

He makes a sound like pity. My fingers tighten on the rail. I let them.

Mick doesn't chase ghosts. He brings facts vet logs. Call records. The vandalism photos. He calls Mr. Whitaker, hair full of hay. "She knows how to pull a calf," he says. "Knows how to wait on a vet without losing the cow. She works."

The judge leans forward. "Miss Campbell, you are young. Why this? Why not return to your work abroad?"

"Because I said I would," I answer. "Because land needs to be kept. Henry taught me that. It doesn't matter if a thing's romantic. It matters if it's right." A sound rises behind me approval or scorn, I don't care. Wendell rises next, full of lineage and sentiment. He tosses the word family around like confetti, but never once looks at me when he says it.

Mick's closing is tough, practical. "Probate isn't heritage right," he says. "It's paper and possession. Intent and execution. Stewardship and standing."

Wendell's solicitor gives his closing like a sermon. Gravity of land. Heritage. Tradition. He never says profit. He doesn't have to.

The judge leans back, paper shuffling. "Brief recess," he says. "We'll reconvene shortly." Recess isn't mercy. It's a delay. But it keeps the blow from landing before I'm squared to receive it.

Chapter Twenty-Nine

Patrick

The judge's voice is sanded down to a neutral tone. "On the matter of standing, the court finds in favor of the petitioner. Mr. Sutton is granted standing. Ms. Campbell will have forty-five days to vacate the premises."

The gavel sounds like a gunshot in the room.

Mharie doesn't move. I feel her stillness like a vacuum. Mick's jaw ticks once; his pencil stops mid-tap. Wendell's mouth twitches smirk dressed up as sympathy then he tips two fingers to the brim of that too new hat and turns for the aisle like he's late to lunch, not carving up someone's life. I stand, step to her left, and hold my ground until the benches clear. Bodies spill around us, the scrape of shoes and the private hum of voices. I put a hand on her elbow. Not guiding. Anchoring. She stands on the first try. Good.

Mick leans in. "We'll move for a stay and notice appeal. I'll have the written order within the hour. We keep our feet under us," Mick says.

"Good," I say. "Because I'm not done."

"Aye," she says. It's almost soundless.

I steer us toward the aisle, shoulder to shoulder with her, so anyone with a camera or a question has to go through me first. Wendell's lawyer glances our way calculating then decides against it. Smart.

"Go," Mick says, quiet. "I'll text when I've got the stamped order. We start filing this afternoon."

I nod. "We'll be at the house."

I get her outside without anyone stopping us. The sky is winter-pale and merciless. We don't say a word as we walk to the truck. She climbs in like a robot, like she's not really with me. I circle to the driver's side, start the engine, and pull away slowly. The courthouse recedes in the mirror, all brick and smug certainty. We drive with the radio off. The quiet is jagged and sharp. Pickups slide by, the feed store sign flashes past, the bakery window is full of cheer despite the bomb that just leveled Mharie's life. She sits with her hands flat on her thighs, breathing too evenly.

"Say it," I tell the road.

"Say what?" She sounds like she's saving herself for later.

"Anything you need to get out before we're home?"

She shakes her head once. "No' here." She swallows. "No' now."

We take the last turn for the county road. Fenceposts tick by like a metronome. Her phone lights in the cupholder with a handful of messages neighbors, Mick's paralegal, Mrs. Ortiz. She turns it face down. At the gate, she gets out, flips the chain, and waves me through. When she climbs back into the cab, her hands are shaking. She hides them in her sleeves. I pretend not to see. The cameras blink as we roll up the drive. The house sits stubbornly against the pale sky, the way it always has, square, honest, unafraid. I kill the engine and the sudden stillness is vicious.

She opens her door and goes inside without waiting for me. I follow. The binder is still on the mantel, tabs crisp, sentinel. She stops in front of it and stands like she's studying a map of a country that just got redrawn.

"Spitfire," I say.

She exhales a laugh that isn't a laugh. "Dinnae call me that just now." Her voice is hoarse. "I'll shatter."

"Then shatter."

That breaks something open. She turns and hits my chest with the sides of both fists not hard, not to hurt, just to register impact against something that won't give. I take it. She keeps breathing like she's drowning standing up.

She's trembling now, her body a live wire of fury and fear, the kind of deep, exhausted grief that comes when someone realizes good work wasn't a shield. She pushes at my chest, a desperate, futile attempt to create space, then grabs my shirt and hauls me down like she means to devour me. "Patrick."

"Yes."

"Make it stop."

I don't ask what it is. I step in, crowd her back into the edge of the couch, take her face in both hands, and kiss her with a ferocity that jars us both. She opens like she's falling and clings like she isn't.

"This?" I ask against her mouth, one final check.

"Aye." It's half curse, half prayer. "Now."

The last of my caution snaps. I lift her, drop to the cushions with her straddling my lap, and she drags my hair, opens her mouth no sweetness, just primal need. She bites my shoulder; I curse; we both breathe like we're surfacing from drowning. I grip the back of her sweater, fist the wool, and she jerks it out of my hand and over her head, chin high, daring me to look and not take. I do both. She yanks at my shirt; buttons scatter. Second shirt in as many days. Fine.

She pushes me back and tears off her pants and underwear, her eyes blazing with a mix of fury and desperation. Her hands roam my chest, tracing the lines of my muscles with a fierce intensity. I can feel the heat radiating from her body, the electric charge of her touch. She leans down, her breath hot against my ear. "I need you to make me forget," she whispers, her voice raw and urgent. "Make me feel something other than this pain."

I respond with a growl, flipping us over so she's beneath me, her body pinned to the couch. My mouth crashes down on hers, a brutal, demanding kiss that leaves us both breathless. She arches up against me, her body pressing into mine, seeking more, always more. I trail kisses down her neck, nipping and sucking at her skin, leaving marks that will linger long after this moment is over.

Her hands tug at my belt, fumbling with the buckle in her haste. I help her, quickly shedding my pants and kicking them aside. She reaches for me, her fingers wrapping around my length, stroking with a fierce, almost punishing grip. I groan, my hips bucking into her touch, my body aching with need.

I pull her hand away, pinning it above her head as I settle between her thighs. She wraps her legs around me, pulling me close, urging me on with a desperate whimper. I enter her in one hard thrust, her body clenching around me, welcoming me in. We move together, our bodies slamming against each other in a frantic, desperate rhythm. The couch creaks and groans beneath us, a symphony to our primal dance.

Her nails rake down my back, leaving trails of fire and desperation. I capture her mouth in a fierce kiss, swallowing her cries as she comes undone beneath me. Her body convulses around me, milking me, pushing me over the edge. I follow her into oblivion, my release tearing through me like a storm.

We collapse together, our bodies slick with sweat, our breaths coming in ragged gasps. She buries her face in my neck, her tears hot against my skin. I hold her close, my arms wrapped tightly around her, anchoring her to me. In this moment, there is no past, no future, only the raw, unfiltered connection of our bodies and the desperate need to escape the storm that rages within.

I feel her heartbeat against my chest. It slows. She breathes a ragged breath that shakes me more than a sob would. I hold her until the tremor leaves her limbs. Then I reach for the throw on the back of the couch and pull it over us both because the house feels colder than it is.

My phone buzzes on the table. A text from Adam: Heard. You okay? Three dots appear. Calling in two.

I text back: *Call now.* Then I message Mick: *Ten minutes.* The phone rings. "Adam."

"Hey, brother." Adam's voice is already edged like he's halfway to work boots and a sledge. "Tell me you didn't just get sandbagged in a courtroom."

"We did."

"Forty-five?"

"Forty-five."

A pause, like he's measuring that number against every room that ever cheated him. "Okay. I'm calling the guy I used in Denver. He already owes me two favors and a drink. If there's anything off with this judge money, golf trips, bowling league dues we're going to have it. I'll handle the retainer."

"You don't need "

"Don't insult me. Family means the check's already cleared." His voice softens by a degree. "How's she holding?"

"She won't quit. So neither will I," I say.

"Good." It's not glee. It's a relief. "Forward me everything. Order, docket, and opposing counsel's name. I'll have the PI start with the financials, then move on to associates. Give me forty-eight hours for a first pass."

"Copy."

"And Patrick?"

"Yeah."

"Loop Brandon," Adam says. "He's chomping at the bit."

I find a smile I didn't expect. "I'll call him after I get her settled."

"Got it. I'll check back tonight. And... tell her she's not alone. She'll hate hearing it. Tell her anyway."

"I will."

We hang up. I set the phone face down and kiss the top of her head. "Adam's on it. PI starts now."

She nods against me. "Aye."

Mick's name pops up. I put him on speaker.

"Orders in," he says. "We'll file the notice today, with the motion for stay. I'd like to get a hearing on the stay within the week."

"Tell me what you need from us. Adam is calling a PI to see what he can dig up," I say.

"Statements from the neighbors who showed up today. No theatrics, no extras. Just truth. And if your brother digs up anything on this judge, loop me in first."

"You'll have it," I say.

"Good. Eat something." He hangs up without a goodbye, because he's already moving onto the next item on his list.

I turn the phone over in my hand and look at her. She looks back. We don't make promises we can't keep today. We don't say always. We say now and mean it all the way down.

Later I'll call Brandon, and we'll start the next fight. Later there will be filings and stays, and whatever Adam digs up like a bone the county hoped no one would find. Later there will be decisions about what home means when a piece of paper tries to tell you it isn't yours.

Right now, I stand, kiss her once, and go check the gates.

When I come back in, she's on the couch under the tartan throw, eyes closed, mug empty on the table, the binder still a sentinel on the mantel. I set the chain on the front door; the lock gives its solid click. She opens her eyes when the sound lands.

"We're not finished," I tell her.

She nods, and the crack in her is still there, but it isn't spreading. "I ken."

"Good." I toe off my boots. "Then come here."

She lifts the blanket. I lay down beside her and gather her in, the two of us facing the fire that's more ember than flame but still enough to heat a room. Outside the day keeps going. Inside, for a little while, we stop the world from getting in.

Tomorrow I'll have a list for the appeal and a call with a PI I've never met. Tomorrow I'll ask Brandon to bring me whatever proof he can carry, and I'll throw it on a table like a gauntlet. Tomorrow will be war.

Today is the break and the burn and the breathing after.

I hold her. The house holds us both. And in the quiet between the ticks of the clock, I swear the place itself says keep going.

Chapter Thirty

Mharie

I wake to a quiet that isna sleep but the space after it. Thin morning light leaks around the curtains. The stove ticks like a clock with a cough. The house smells of ash and wool and something sweet from the shortbread tin we left open.

There's a ridge where my cheek pressed the couch seam. My neck protests when I sit up. The tartan throw slides to my lap. Across the room, the binder sits on the mantel, square and certain, tabbed like a hymnbook. HIGHLAND HOMESTEAD EVIDENCE. I hate it and love it in the same breath.

I don't look at the doorway to the hall. I don't know where he is or isna. I pull the throw tight and stand.

The floorboards know me. They complain in the places Henry never bothered to fix. The window over the sink is pale with frost. Outside, the pasture has the color of old tin. No new snow. Just a hard white edge along the rail and the trough rim.

Dougal stands by the near fence, shag frozen in clumps like he's been sculpted by a child with cold hands. He looks wronged, which is his favorite sport.

I set the kettle and collect the treacle tin and the wee tub of salt. I line up two mugs because my hands need something that obeys. The pilot catches with a soft pop. Flame, then patience. Steam when it's ready. That's all.

I keep my eyes on the blue tongue of fire and make a list in my head like a prayer: Mick wants statements. Mrs. Ortiz will give one. Dale will too. The Whitakers, if I go myself and ask at their kitchen door. The vet can write an affidavit to go with the log already in the binder. I'll call the feed store to get their clerk to confirm the invoices we've filed. I'll print fresh trail-cam timestamps and staple them to the packet for the appeal so nothing gets lost between a desk and a man with a pen.

I do not let my mind say forty-five. It tries. It scratches at the inside of my ribs like a trapped thing. I set the mugs closer to the stove just to feel the small victory of heat on my fingers.

When the kettle begins to fuss, I cut it off before the whistle, the way Henry taught me. Don't wake what ye don't need. Treacle in each, a whisper of salt, water to the line on the pottery I've learned by heart. I leave one mug by the stove. I take mine and the lock key and go out the back door before the house can remember how to hold me.

Cold takes the breath quick. The yard is stiff with it. The floodlights are off, but the cameras blink their wee red lights. I pull the door tight until the latch bites, then turn the key. The click is louder than it should be. Tea burns the roof of my mouth. I welcome it. Dougal lifts his head at the sound. He swings it like he's showing off horns he polished overnight. Then he huffs, a great discontented sound, and lumbers to the near gate with that walk that looks like swagger until ye ken he's just big and honest about it. He stops with his nose at the wire panel and blows a mist that smells of hay and old rain.

"Morning, Your Majesty," I tell him. My voice scrapes. "Ye've opinions, do ye?"

He shoves the panel with his forehead. It clacks against the post. I can see where a new brace went on last week clean wood against grey. The sight is a small balm and a small knife. Dougal noses again, then does a thing he never quite does when I've not got a carrot. He sticks his tongue out and tries to curl it over the panel to reach my mug. It's ridiculous. It's daft. It's so deliberate an attempt to make me swear that a sound bursts out of me before I can shut it half laugh, half something else.

"Ye great beast," I manage, stepping closer. "It's tea, no' molasses."

He huffs. A strand of clover from last night's hay sticks to his whiskers. He goes still, then does a small, awkward hop with his front feet like a bairn trying new boots. Another huff. He tries the tongue again. Failure. He looks offended by physics.

I set the mug on the porch rail and lean my shoulder against the post. "I ken," I tell him, quietly. "I ken what ye're doing."

He knows something's wrong. He can smell it. He can smell rain in July and rot in lumber and the fox long before I see his tail. He smells me now salt and fear and whatever ache lives in the place just under the breastbone where vows go to sleep.

"This isna fair," I say to a cow who understands more than men do. The words shake loose. "It's no' even law. It's a story folk like better."

He blinks at me as if he'll accept a carrot instead of justice.

"I did the work." The heat in the words isna anger; it's a fever. "I did every bloody thing right. I came back."

He butts the panel softer. The chain rattles. There's hay stuck to his lashes. He looks absurd. Holy. Both.

"I ken," I say again. "I hear ye."

He bends his enormous head and presses it against my shoulder until I have to plant my feet. Heat against my collarbone. Breath clouding the air. His skull weighs like a vow. He's careful with it.

"Ye're going tae ruin my jumper," I tell him into shag. My voice finds a quieter place. "A fine help ye are."

He sighs. The sound is ancient. We stand like that until my arms chill and my hands go numb and my head clears.

Inside I reheat the tea that had cooled and take the first swallow too fast. It burns again. Good. I breathe in the steam like medicine.

I do not look at the couch. I do not look at the door to the hall. There is nothing in any of that that will help on a day like this.

At the sink, my reflection is hair like I lost a fight with a thistle, eyes too bright and too dark both. I don't look long. I don't want my own face to start talking to me.

A crow lands on the fence post and cocks its head like it's ready to judge my next twenty moves. I nod like I'll take his counsel under advisement. He blinks slowly. He's no' on my side, but he's honest. It'll do.

I check the locks. Then the back door, the mudroom, the cellar latch, the crossbar on the porch gate because doing the same small thing twice sometimes fools the panic into sitting down.

When I pass the mantel, my fingers brush the binder tabs as if the plastic was skin that needed calming. Daft. It helps anyway.

No radio. I've no stomach for cheerful men who say "holidays" like it fixes anythin'. The stove ticks. The wind lifts the eaves. The house keeps its old secrets, but none of them feel like they'll eat me today. I'll take that too.

The phone buzzes and makes me jump anyway. Habit, fear, both. I flip it over without opening. Three names I ken and one I don't. I let them sit. I'm no' a clerk today. I'm the ground.

More tea. Back door. Palm on the cool glass. Fog blooms where my skin warms it. Outside, Dougal paws at a muddy patch he likely saved for just such a day. He finds a single thistle head under the crusted frost and shakes it until the seeds fly like snow that forgot how to be beautiful. He tosses his head like he meant it as a speech.

"Fine," I say, and my mouth turns before I can stop it. "Philosopher."

The sun makes a thin liar of the frost. The porch step holds when I put weight on it. The hinge shrieks when I swing the gate. I should hate that sound. I don't. It's a warning and a promise at once.

I walk the fence without thinking and with all my thoughts. Cameras blink. The wee tacks to catch headlights gleam where the sun canna reach. The lower shed lock takes the key on the first try. Open, check, close, test. Fight in my fingers, steadiness too. They don't cancel each other out. I didna know that was possible.

At the barn bench, I let the tea sit in my hands and finally say the word that's been trying to break me.

"Forty-five," I say to the yard, and it doesna ring, just drops like scrap iron onto the dirt. "Forty-five days."

It's not a spell. Not a curse. It's a measure. A rude one. But if time is a yardstick, I can use it too.

Forty-five days is six weeks and a scrap. Enough to file and stand and file again. Enough to decide whether I'm staying forever which I'm no' doing today or leaving for a while which I'm no' doing today either. Enough to hold the ache and the stubbornness and do the work that belongs to me without letting a man's clean hat and cologne tell me what my life is.

I finish the tea and set the mug beside me. This isna fair, I think again, but softer. Not a shout. A truth laid flat.

It's no' law. Not the kind I was taught. It's a story the kind men tell at barbecues and on benches about who should have what because of who their uncle's uncle was. I can't make them stop telling it. I can make a better one and hand it to a clerk who canna pretend it isna there.

I stand because sitting willna get the list done. Inside I relock the door, hang the key on the tiny hook where it belongs, and return to the table.

Paper. Pen. Names. "Mrs. Ortiz school schedule to verify morning sightings." "Dale truck delivery slips, signatures." "Whitaker calf date/time, weather, vet ETA."

I write "Henry" and stop because there's nothing to write except memory and the way he said my name when I was fifteen and so angry I could have set the world alight. I put a line through it, hate that, write it again, leave it plain. If I go, it'll be because that's right for the fight, no' because I'm bleeding. If I stay, it'll be because this is the work, no' because I'm stubborn and scared of being a lass who leaves. I say it out loud because sometimes my mouth believes my voice more than my mind.

Somewhere by the cedars, Dougal bellows with theatre that says he's hungry and ready to tell the whole county. I let him talk a minute longer than I should. Then I set the list under the treacle tin so it won't slide and go feed my philosopher, because even if the county prefers stories to work, the work doesna stop for its opinion. On the porch, I set the chain, open the gate, and let the hinge scream for both of us. Dougal meets me like he's never been fed in his born days. I thump his flank with the heel of my hand, and he leans into it shamelessly. The hay bale gives with a grunt. I pitch flakes clean. I stand and watch him tear into it, as if joy were still allowed.

"Aye," I tell the pasture and the cameras and the cold. "We keep going."

Chapter Thirty-One

Patrick

I wake before dawn, throat dry, jaw aching like I've been arguing in my sleep. Two days since the verdict, and the house still feels like it's holding its breath. Yesterday I stayed out of her way and buried myself in the spare room with the laptop, tracing Wendell's trail through filings, calls, and handshakes. I can't fix the hurt, but I can even the fight. Somewhere in the dark, Dougal shifts his weight and snorts like he's dreaming about outrunning gravity. I roll out of bed and pull on flannel and boots that still smell of hay.

Outside, frost rims the grass, silver as guilt. The cameras blink steadily red, quiet witnesses that don't lie or sleep. Dougal sees me and comes lumbering over, breath puffing like a train. "Morning, trouble," I mutter, pitching flakes of hay into the ring. He dives in like he hasn't eaten in days.

I check the porch crossbar, then swing the gate wide. The hinge screams. I let it. Noise is proof. When I drop the bar back into place, the silence that follows feels earned.

Inside I scrawl a list on a feed slip.

— Call Adam: update, PI brief, next target list.

— Call Brandon: ground game, travel window.

— Mick: stay timeline, neighbor statements.

— Hardware store: locks, motion lights, signage.

— Trail-cam battery swap.

— Print photo sets w/ timestamps.

— Ortiz, Dale, Whitakers—statements.

— Lock audit: cellar, mudroom, parlor.

I slap the slip under the longhorn magnet on the fridge and call Adam. He answers before the second ring. "Morning."

"PI turn up anything yet?" I ask.

"Breadcrumbs," he says. "Judge's golfing circle—one of the names ties back to Wendell's buddy. Could be noise, could be rot. I'm digging."

"Keep at it. Send me anything that smells off."

"Already in your inbox." Paper shuffles; a chair creaks. "And Pat—don't let her carry this by herself. She'll try."

"She won't have to."

"Good. Keep me looped on the stay filing. I'll keep pressure on the PI."

"Copy that."

We hang up. Brandon picks up on the third ring, wind in the receiver and the faint sound of a gate chain rattling. "You sound like a man about to ask me for a favor."

"I am. You still got friends at the VFW?"

"Couple. You want eyes or trouble?"

"Start with eyes. Judge plays a weekly foursome—same crew every Saturday. The PI flagged one of 'em. See what you can turn up."

"I'll make a few calls. If it smells dirty, I'll fly down tomorrow."

"Bring coffee."

"Already packed," he says, a grin in his voice I can hear but not see. "See you tomorrow."

The line goes dead. Typical Brandon short on words, long on follow through. I trust him to land hard and quietly. That's how we were raised to fix things by showing up, not talking about it. For a moment, it's just the wind outside and the low hum of the fridge. The kind of silence that follows when every man you trust is already moving and you're the one left holding the ground. The kettle clicks on its own timer, a small domestic proof that something in this house still answers when asked. I pour two mugs out of habit, set hers by the stove to stay warm. My hands keep doing ordinary things while my head lines up the next battle.

I text Mick: What do you need?

 He replies a minute later: Keep your originals. I need the hard copies for filing signatures, timestamps, everything with ink. And if Adam's PI digs up anything, print that too. Judges respect paper more than pixels.

Copy, I text back. You'll have it by morning.

The sun's up by the time the list's half checked off. I need motion. Motion means I'm not thinking. By midmorning, I'm in town loading hardware: new hasp, two deadbolts, motion floods, three *No Trespassing* signs because sometimes words scare faster than fences. Back at the homestead, the light's brighter, but the cold hasn't quit. I replace the deadbolt on the mudroom door, install the hasp on the cellar, and mount the motions where they'll catch a shadow crossing the yard. When I test them, the glare burns doubt clean for a second.

The trail-cam battery dies mid-swap, but I still get two new units up on the lower fence line. Angled right this time, fewer blind spots. I snap a photo of each install and email it to myself with the timestamp. Paper trail, proof of presence. Mrs. Ortiz waves me in when I knock. Flour on her hands, eyes sharp. She writes her statement in perfect teacher script, hands it over, and gives a look that says *keep her safe* louder than words. Dale at the feed store prints the slips I need, circles delivery times, and makes me sign for them "so the clerk doesn't get cute." I do.

Each page feels like another stone in a wall.

By the time I'm back, the kitchen table's half-covered in paper. I label the backs in pen, staple the photos, and stack them neatly. Mick's going to want order; he'll have it. The back door opens. She's there hair wind-tangled, cheeks flushed, Dougal's slobber on her sleeve.

"You've been out," I say.

"So have ye." Her voice is steadier than her eyes. "The hinges scream properly now. I heard them from the barn."

"That's the sound of home keeping watch."

She almost smiles, then points at the stack on the table. "Is that all of it?"

"For today."

She runs her fingers along the edge of the binder like she's checking its pulse. "I spoke to Mrs. Ortiz. She said you'd been by."

"She's a force of nature."

"Aye." She breathes in deep, sets her shoulders. "Thank you."

"For what?"

"For no' talking at me like I'll break."

"I wouldn't dare."

The kettle clicks off behind me. I pour the tea, slide one mug toward her. She takes it with both hands, and for a heartbeat, the world remembers how to be quiet.

"Adam's digging," I tell her. "Brandon's coming tomorrow. Mick wants the supplemental packet on his desk by noon. We've got momentum."

She stares into the steam. "It doesna feel like it yet."

"It will."

She nods, then looks toward the window where Dougal stands chewing glory out of a patch of hay. "He's been trying to make me laugh."

"Seems he's better at it than I am."

"Ye dinnae try. That's why it works."

We drink the rest in silence. The house breathes around us—wood settling, wind tugging at the porch, fire popping softly in the grate. It isn't peace, not really. It's recovery disguised as routine.

When her cup's empty, she sets it down and presses a thumbprint into the ring it leaves, like she's sealing something invisible. "Forty-three days," she says quietly.

"Plenty of time to build something worth keeping," I answer.

She studies me for a long moment. "Promise ye'll keep me in the room when it matters."

"I promise."

As she passes, her hand trails along my arm, a quiet promise grounded in touch.

I set the chain after her, check the lock twice, and write one more line on the feed-slip pinned to the fridge: *Stand our ground.*

The ink bleeds a little, but the message stays.

Chapter Thirty-Two

Mharie

The morning doesn't ease in it erupts.

Dougal's bawl shakes the windowpanes before the kettle even thinks about warming, followed by a sharp shout a man's, high and horrified, like a goose being mugged. I grab my jumper off the chair, jam my feet into boots, and run for the porch.

A stranger is halfway up the lane, flapping his arms as though invisible hornets are after him. Dougal lumbers behind at his usual glacial gallop, tail swishing, convinced he's found a new friend who happens to be bad at standing still. The camera light on the fence blinks steadily, catching every tragic second.

"Dougal!" I call. "He's no' a snack!"

The man a reporter, judging by the dangling camera and city shoes sprints the last few yards and scrambles onto the hood of his rental car. Dougal stops short, lets out a satisfied huff, and tilts his great head. You can almost see the thought forming: *where'd the treat go?*

I walk down the path, breath puffing white. "You're trespassing," I tell him. "He's friendly till he isna."

"He charged me!" the reporter squeaks.

"He trotted enthusiastically," I correct. "Different crime."

The poor soul clutches his camera strap like a rosary. "I was just getting a few establishing shots the paper wanted a human-interest piece "

Dougal snorts loud enough to rattle the car door. The man squeals and dives inside. The engine coughs, wheels spit gravel, and he fishtails down the drive like he's escaping a siege.

I turn to my defender, who blinks at the retreating car with deep bovine satisfaction. "Well done," I tell him. "Defender of the realm. Terror of journalists."

He swings his head, nearly knocking me off balance with a nudge that could pass for affection or apology. "Aye, aye, easy now. Back to your kingdom."

He pretends not to hear. I grab the nearest broom from the porch and herd him along the lane, boots sliding on frost. He ambles like repentance in motion slow, enormous, entirely unbothered. The fence gate stands wide where he must've lifted the latch again. Clever bastard.

"Ye think ye're Houdini with horns, don't ye?" I mutter, fixing the chain back through its loop. Dougal eyes me sidelong, then noses the pocket of my coat until he finds a treat I didn't mean to carry. He takes it delicately, lips tickling my palm.

"That's bribery, not forgiveness," I tell him, even as my mouth softens into something dangerously close to fondness.

When he's back behind the fence and the gate secured with the extra clasp Patrick added last week, I rest a hand on his shaggy forehead. "Stay put this time."

He exhales slow through his nose, enough to warm my sleeve, then turns away to the hay like I've ceased to exist. Typical.

Back in the kitchen, laughter ambushes me before I can stop it. It rolls out, helpless, the kind that leaves salt at the corners of your eyes. The kettle trills impatiently; I pour my cuppa. Steam curls up and, for a heartbeat, I let myself enjoy it warmth, absurdity, proof the world hasn't stolen everything yet.

I jot a note for Patrick on the pad by the phone:

A reporter came by. He survived. Dougal claimed victory. Added another sign.

The ink smudges where I laugh again. Small mercies.

Outside, I hammer the fresh *NO TRESPASSING* sign into frozen ground beside the gate. The metal bite of the hammer steadies me. Work always does.

The rest of the morning unfolds as it should. Feed for Dougal and his ladies. Check the floodlights. A short call with Mick about the hearing schedule; his voice is crisp, determined.

"Forty-two days left, Campbell. Let's make them count."

"Aye," I answer. "We already are."

The wind comes meaner by noon, sliding under the porch boards. I eat standing up cheese, bread, last of the jam and watch Dougal chew glory out of the hay pile like nothing in the world could touch him. Maybe he's right.

At the lower fence line, the cameras blink their patient language. One winks as I pass, a small electronic nod. The yard feels awake guarding, maybe even proud.

I hear the truck door slam before I see him. Patrick's voice carries from the barn, low and measured. He's been fixing something, maybe everything. He doesn't call my name, and I don't go to him. We work side by side in different rooms, two halves of a shared vow: hold the line.

By afternoon, the clouds build muscle. I check the gate latch, the porch hinge, and the cellar hasp. Everything holds. Dougal trails after me like an overgrown dog, tail flicking snow onto my boots.

When the wind picks up, I lean against his shoulder for balance. He makes a sound deep in his chest, somewhere between a sigh and a sermon.

"You've done your good deed," I tell him. "No more reporters today."

He flicks an ear, unconvinced.

Inside, the house is warmer than it's been since the verdict. The stove ticks. The air smells of iron and tea and old paper. On the table, the binder waits square, certain, patient. I glance at it but let it be. There's something better to do than catalog worry.

I spread a clean sheet of paper and write across the top:
Things Still Ours.

– Dougal's laugh, if he had one.

– The hinge that screams honest.

– The neighbors who show up without being asked.

– The ground under our boots.

I pin it to the corkboard above the sink, where the sun can find it later. Lists are spells of a sort; this one feels like protection.

Toward dusk, the air sharpens until the porch steps squeal under frost. I light the lamps Henry's way dark corners first then make another mug of tea. Outside, Dougal bellows, satisfied with his own echo. He's earned his supper, so I take him a second flake of hay. The sky bruises purple; the cameras blink like tiny heartbeats. Patrick comes in as I'm hanging up my coat.

He smells of sawdust and cold air. We pass each other in the narrow hall. His hand grazes my back a touch not of ownership but alignment.

"A reporter came up the lane this morning," I add as I hang up my coat.

"I saw the new sign," he says, brows lifting. "Dougal behave?"

"Depends on your definition," I answer. "He chased the poor man onto his car." His mouth twitches. "You all right?"

"Aye," I say. "Just one more thing we'll need to stay ahead of."

I nod once. He nods back. A small country with a working treaty.

At the table, a new note waits in his square handwriting:

Stay hearing = Thursday. Brandon at dawn. Adam says: keep receipts + ink.

The last line is underlined twice. It makes me smile despite everything; only a man from Willow Glen could sound like every Scottish mother I've ever known in so few words. *Keep receipts.*

I write beneath it: Aye. And keep the ground. Then I draw a box around both, as if a pencil could make a promise stronger.

Later, after the dishes, after the quiet, I stand at the window. The yard gleams with frost, the new sign catching light from the motion lights. Somewhere near the cedar, Dougal snorts and shifts, sentinel again. The gate hinge sings once, pure and defiant. I smile into the dark.

"Tomorrow," I tell the glass, "we go faster."

The wind answers low, steady, like an old hymn that still remembers the tune.

The floor creaks behind me. I don't turn right away. He comes up beside me, close enough that our reflections blur together in the window glass.

"Reporter's alive?" he asks.

"Barely."

A smile ghosts his mouth. "Dougal's becoming a local legend."

"Better him than us."

He slips an arm around my shoulders, slow and certain, the kind of touch that feels less like claiming and more like remembering. For a long moment we just watch the yard breathe the frost, the lights, the stubborn cow that won the morning.

When he finally speaks, his voice is soft. "Tomorrow," he says, echoing me.

"Aye," I whisper. "We go faster."

Chapter Thirty-Three

Patrick

Dawn hasn't decided what it wants yet when tires crunch over the cattle guard at the end of the lane. Headlights skate across the porch. A door thunks, firm and familiar. I'm already halfway there when the knock lands.

Brandon stands on the step in a canvas jacket, eyes red from the night, duffel on one shoulder, thermos in the other hand.

"You called. I came," he says, voice gravel and jet-lagged.

"You flew."

"Red-eye into Austin, rental straight here. Coffee's terrible." He tips the thermos.

"You'll survive."

We clasp forearms our version of a hug and I wave him in.

Inside, the kitchen table is a crime scene of paper and ink: the PI's spreadsheet, golf-club roster, a diagram of shell entities with one name circling back too many times. I push the newest stack toward him.

"Same name in three places," I say. "Member dues at the club, a 'consulting' check into a shell, and Wendell's buddy signing off on a county contract."

Brandon whistles low, already rolling his shoulders loose like a fighter warming up. "That's not a coincidence. That's leverage." He sets the thermos down, flips open a notebook. "My guy's at the Dallas field office. We don't go local; we go fed. You good with that?"

"I'm good with fast and clean."

He nods, thumbs a quick text. "I'll tee this as a confidential tip with supporting docs. But we need a tight chain-of-custody." He taps the table. "Ink over pixels. Originals in a folder. Copies for us. Timeline summary with citations."

I slide the envelope of hard copies to him. "Already pulled."

He grins without showing teeth. "You're learning."

We work in quiet. He reads fast, marks cleaner, and organizes the mess into lanes: Money. Access. Motive. We strip out anything we can't prove and leave the rest to stand on its own legs. The house wakes around us stove ticking, pipes giving their old-man cough, wind testing the eaves. Out in the yard, Dougal bawls once like he's announcing we have company, then goes back to pretending hay is the answer to every problem.

By the time the thin light finds the window over the sink, we've got a clean packet: cover sheet, bulleted timeline, exhibits tabbed. Brandon lays his palm on the stack like he's checking a pulse.

"This will move," he says. "Even if the judge doesn't topple right away, he's going to feel heat."

Bootsteps cross the porch; the back door latch clicks. Mharie comes in with the cold on her cheeks and a braid down her back, Dougal's slobber drying in a comet across her sleeve. She clocks Brandon, then the table.

"You're building a taller wall," she says.

"That's the idea," I answer.

She studies the tabs Money, Access, Motive like she could lift them with her hands. "Good. The sea doesna scare easily. We dinna either."

Brandon's mouth tips. "Morning, Campbell."

"Brandon." She pours tea, sets a spare mug by the stove without looking at either of us, and leaves us to it. The hinge sings as the door swings. Treaty intact.

We keep going. Brandon calls his contact and speaks a language of initials and sections, measured and careful.

"Anonymous source is fine," he says into the phone. "But we're providing copies of checks, membership rolls, and a map of the shells. No editorial. Just proof... Yeah. Email for intake, physical drop where you want it. Today if you can staff it."

He hangs up, scribbles an address. "Dallas wants the packet scanned to their intake address and a hard set delivered to a satellite desk in Austin by the end of the day. They'll route internally public corruption squad."

"Adam's going to want to bless the chain."

"Texted him wheels-down," he says, showing me the already-blue bubble. "He's on board. He'll have his GC eyes on the cover letter in an hour."

We build the cover: simple, declarative, no speeches. Alleged pattern of improper financial relationship between seated county judge and petitioner-adjacent parties. Attached exhibits A through H. Suggested lines of inquiry: travel, dues, gifts, undisclosed income, recusal history.

I staple, then sign the index. My name looks steadier on paper than I feel in my chest. Brandon reads it once more, then nudges the pen back to me.

"Initial each exhibit tab," he says. "If anyone ever questions what was left in this room, we can swear to the exact stack."

"Paranoid," I say, doing it anyway.

"Prepared," he corrects. "And this," he holds up the golf roster with the circled name, "is the thread they'll pull first."

A shadow crosses the window. Dougal parks himself like a shaggy sentinel and fogs the glass with his opinion. Brandon snorts.

"He still thinks he's a dog?"

"He thinks everyone is a carrot," I say.

"Fair." He lines the pages square and taps them into a manila folder. "Austin drop. I'll go. It's my mess to start; let me carry it."

"Take the copy. I'll keep the originals in the binder until we hear back."

He tips his thermos toward me. "You going to tell her?"

"When the packet's out of our hands." I glance at the hall. "We don't promise results. We promise work."

"That's why she chose you."

I don't answer. He doesn't make me. We move to logistics instead route to Austin, weather on the pass, a gas station in between that still prints receipts with time stamps big enough to read without squinting. Brandon adds a line to the cover sheet: Contact info for follow-up (counsel). He lists Mick and Adam; he leaves me off. Smart.

Mid-morning, the printer coughs out the last of the scanned pages. Brandon seals the Austin set with tape from the junk drawer, writes the field address in block letters a clerk can't pretend to misread. I slip the originals into our binder new tab:

Federal Packet and slide it back onto the mantel, square and plain like a promise you could stand on.

Mharie returns, sets a plate of bread and cheese on the table like we didn't notice we were starving. She doesn't ask for an update. She takes one look at the sealed envelope and nods like a woman who recognizes a line being thrown from a boat to a man who can't swim yet but refuses to drown.

"Bring it back empty," she says to Brandon.

"Yes, ma'am." The corners of his eyes soften. "You need anything from town?"

"Justice," she says, straight, no smile.

"Working on it." He tucks the packet under his arm and turns to me. "You staying put?"

"I'll hold the ground."

"Good." He claps my shoulder once. "Text when Mick confirms the stay hearing slot. I'll be back by dark."

We step onto the porch together. The cold bites clean. Across the yard, Dougal lifts his head, chews, and decides we're not interesting enough to interrupt lunch. Brandon squints down the lane like he can see Austin from here.

"Proud of you," he says, almost offhand. "Not for the paper. For how you're holding her."

"That's your official stance?"

"That's the brother stance." He grins, then heads for the rental, engine turning over into a low hum. Gravel pops under the tires; frost fractures in a soft crackle. He taps the horn one short note and is gone.

I stand until the sound bleeds out of the morning. The yard breathes. The hinge on the gate complains when the wind tests it and then shuts itself again, stubborn as a mule. Inside, the kettle's already pushing toward a boil. I pour a mug and set it by the stove for her, out of habit and because it helps.

When she comes in this time, she stops beside me instead of passing through. She looks at the space on the table where the envelope was and then at my hands wrapped around the mug.

"Out?" she asks.

"On the road to Austin."

She lets out a breath that trembles at the end, just once, and then it's gone. "Good."

I offer the mug. She takes it, our fingers brushing in the transfer. Heat moves skin to skin, uncomplicated.

"We're not finished," I say.

"I ken," she answers, and for the first time since the verdict, there's something like a glint under the tiredness in her eyes. "The sea doesna scare easily."

"Neither do we."

Her mouth tilts. "Aye. Help me check the lower hinge. The wind's gotten ideas."

We go out together into the thin day, shoulder to shoulder, the gate screaming our boundaries to anyone with ears. At the same time, the cameras blink their patient language and the ground stays under us because we keep telling it to.

Chapter Thirty-Four

Mharie

The courthouse smells of lemon polish and paper, like someone tried to scrub a conscience and left the scent behind. It's been one day since Brandon flew in with the federal contact and Patrick handed over the federal packet. This morning, the wind came in off the flats mean as a snake, and still I button my good wool coat the one Henry bought the last winter before he passed. I pin my hair off my face and walk up these steps like they weren't built to make a lass feel small.

Mick meets me at the door, file under his arm, jaw set. "They're here."

I nod. Patrick's a quiet heat at my back close enough that if the hallway tilts I'll find a solid wall, far enough that I can walk on my own feet.

Inside Mick's office sit two people who are not from here and dinna pretend otherwise. Their badges lie face-up on the table like extra vertebrae. FBI stamped across both in letters that don't care how the county pronounces your surname. The woman's hair is braided tight as purpose; the man's suit looks like it cost him a fight with a tailor. Their coffee's gone cold, and their eyes are very awake.

"Agent Hall," the woman says, offering her hand. "Agent Morales. Thank you for meeting us on short notice. "We were already in Austin reviewing the intake packet; your attorney asked for an in-person interview."

"I'm no' here for courtesy," I tell her, taking the chair opposite. "I'm here for truth."

Her mouth clicks at the corner, the sound of someone appreciating the absence of small talk. "That's our brand."

Mick closes the door, flips the sign to IN CONFERENCE, and sets the file down with neat authority that makes my lungs work better. "You have what my clients compiled," he says. "What else do you need?"

"We'll walk through it in sequence," Hall answers, already uncapping a pen. "Tell us if anything reads wrong."

Patrick stands near the window, the way men do when they mean to guard a thing and still let it speak. The winter light cuts a clean line along his jaw. He never fidgets. He never has to.

Agent Morales passes me a copy of the summary like a teacher handing over a test you already know the answers to. "Wire transfers to a family LLC," he says, tapping. "Golf-trip receipts with overlapping dates. A club dues note squared by a third party."

"Third party being Wendell's pal with the pretty hat," I say, voice flat.

Hall's brows climb. "He's bold."

"Or stupid," I mutter.

"Both tend to travel together," she replies, a dry light in her eyes that says she's seen worse and better both.

They move methodically. Brandon's packet sits in the center like a hub with sensible spokes: club rosters, foursome rotations, the PI's photographs of handshakes by the river where men pretend deals look like friendship. Adam's emails read crisp, almost military *Keep receipts + ink*, underlined twice. We did. We have.

"Trail-cam timestamps?" Morales asks.

"Printed, signed, labeled," Mick says, sliding the stack across. "Original SD cards preserved."

Hall nods. "Thank you." She glances at me. "Ms. Campbell, you're prepared for this to be public?"

"I'd have shouted it from the courthouse roof if I thought the wind would carry it true," I say. "If you bring charges, I'll stand with my name on it. No' a whisper a statement."

Something in Hall's gaze eases at the edges. Not pity calculation. "Then we're aligned," she says. "We don't do whispers."

We keep on; names, dates, checks that match the weekends Wendell posted pictures of borrowed glory. Hall circles three entries. "These are our anchors," she says. "We'll start here."

"Will it be quick?" I ask, hating the thread of hope in it.

Morales shakes his head, honest. "It'll be correct."

"That'll do," I say.

By noon, the coffee's still cold and the room smells of ink and something bright you can't file under evidence. Hall caps her pen. "We'll take this to Austin," she says. "We'll liaise with our federal prosecutor. You'll hear from us."

"Soon?" The word tastes unreliable as the weather.

"Soon," she repeats, and this time it sounds like intent.

We stand. Handshakes again. Morales tucks the file into a case I don't doubt he'd fight a bear for. Hall nods to Mick. "Counselor."

"Agent."

At the door, Hall turns back to me. "You did the work. Don't let anyone tell you different."

"I won't," I say, and manage not to look at Patrick when I do.

The hallway looks the same faded runner, bulletin board, a potted plant that's survived three winters but it doesn't *feel* the same. Something's shifted, like a floor that's been jacked true under your feet. You only notice because now the step lands clean.

Reporters hover by the stairwell in coats too thin for Texas' brand of cold. The agents go first, and a path opens. One man lifts his chin to ask a question without earning it. I shake my head the tiniest fraction. He lets it fall. The red light on his camera blinks but doesn't bite.

Mick locks his office, exhales. "You did fine."

"I did the work," I say. "Now it's their turn."

We take the back stairs, the ones with paint worn down to the lead Henry would've clucked at. Outside the wind cuts sharply off the fields, snapping at flags and the sandwich board that says NO PARKING COURT DAY like the letters offended it.

Across the street, Mrs. Ortiz lifts a hand from the school steps. She doesn't cross she's got kids to wrangle but her look is a prayer with its sleeves rolled. I lift my chin. That's all the liturgy we need.

We don't speak till we're three steps from the truck. Then Patrick says, "Hungry?"

"I could eat," I admit, realizing my stomach's been braced since dawn like it expected a blow.

We make it as far as the cab before his phone buzzes. He glances down, screen glow pale against the frost glare. A small smile hooks one corner of his mouth.

"Adam," he says. "PI's widening the circle two new names tied to Wendell's crowd."

"Good," I say, leaning back in the seat. "About time the tide took someone else for a swim."

"He says to keep receipts," Patrick adds, dry.

I huff a laugh. "That man could put a sermon on an invoice."

He starts the truck. Gravel pops under the tires, wind clawing at the mirrors. The road home waits the kind that doesn't care what news you bring, only that you keep driving.

The radio pushes new-year optimism between cattle futures and a sale on chainsaws. I click it off. The quiet sits easier now not a void, a field lying fallow on purpose.

We pass the feed store. Dale's out front, hat low, arm up in a two-fingered salute that says *I heard* without making a parade of it. The bakery window's full of iced stars shaped by toddlers learning geometry. I make a note to buy two dozen when the craving hits; the county survives by keeping small shops open and gossip busy.

At the home place, the cameras blink their honest little eyes. The gate hinge screams when we swing it ugly and sweet as a truth nobody can ignore. Dougal bawls from the pasture with the drama of a saint set to low comedy, demanding either supper or applause.

He comes at the trot he calls a run, shag lifted by the wind, breath fogging in fat puffs. He stops short and noses the panel where I stand a gentle pressure that could knock a smaller woman backward. I plant my boots. He huffs, generous as ever, and gifts me a face full of hay perfume.

"There she is," Patrick says behind me not to me exactly, but in a way that settles in my stomach and warms there.

We fall into the ordinary. I pitch hay; he checks the lock on the lower shed. The flood at the porch clicks once and flares, as if it remembers its job. The wind tries to get teeth into my scarf and fails. Some part of me that untied itself in Mick's office ties back together on the swing of the gate.

The house feels alive when we step in warm, ticking, something baking even though we didn't light the oven. Maybe relief smells a little like old paper and iron gone soft. Patrick drops the files on the table and leans his hips against the counter.

"You still hungry?"

"Starved," I admit.

He finds what's left of the bread and cuts it thick, butter dull and stubborn in the cold. We share it straight off the board, crumbs scattering like proof we're still here.

"I've got to swing by the print shop Mick wants clean certified copies." he says when we're done. "Then check the gate on my way back."

"Dougal's been testing it again," I warn.

"Then he and I will have words."

There's laughter under it soft, tired, but real. The kind you can build on.

The phone hums again. A message from Mick: Thursday at 10 a.m. is confirmed. Opposing counsel acknowledged receipt.

A car hesitates at the end of the lane press, by the look of the rental decal. The engine idles too long, exhaust curling pale in the cold, then it reverses and disappears.

When Patrick comes back, his hair's wild from the wind and he smells of sawdust and that faint electric edge he gets when the day answers him back instead of fighting just to fight. He sets the envelope from the print shop on the table, kisses my temple without asking because he doesn't need to and says, "Morales called. They're in Austin already. The evidence is moving."

Moving. The syllables land somewhere between my ribs and the tired muscle in my jaw I didn't know I'd been clenching. I sit because the chair is there and because the floor would be a declaration I don't want to make.

"Good," I say and it's a small word that opens a massive door.

We lay the new prints beside the old as if we're building a walkway across mud. Dates line up with dates.

"Forty days," Patrick says quietly, as if he doesn't want to scare the number.

"Forty days," I agree, and feel no heat in it.

The sun drops fast this time of year, like it's late for something better. The sky goes the bruised purple it loves, and the cameras blink like steady hearts. I pull on my boots and go out with a final flake for the king. He meets me at the panel, shag haloed, eyes foolish-holy. I lay a hand against his cheek, warm under the winter.

"Defender of the realm," I tell him. "We're nearly there."

Patrick's already lit the lamps in Henry's order corners first so the shadows don't get ideas. He holds out a mug; I take it, and we stand like people who've been at sea long enough to mistrust land and are learning it again. When he sets his palm at the small of my back, it's not a claim. It's a compass.

Outside the wind shifts and the gate hinge sings once, clear and defiant. I smile into my tea and let the day end without asking it for one thing more.

Chapter Thirty-Five

Patrick

The smell of wood smoke gets me before the light does. It's not the kind that wakes a man gently; it's the kind that reminds you the stove nearly went out in the night and you'd better fix it before the house notices. I stir the embers, feed them kindling, and set the kettle on. Footsteps thump on the porch heavy, familiar, and too early for visitors. The door creaks, and Brandon leans in, jacket zipped to his throat, steam lifting off him like he's carried half the morning chill inside.

"Generator's humming again," he says, rubbing his hands. "Coffee ready?"

"Just about." I pour him a mug, black and too strong. He drinks half before speaking again.

"Trail-cam picked up fresh movement on the south line last night figured Mick would want the prints. Phone was buzzing out by the fence Mick sent word. Austin's pushing through the last of the paperwork. Should move quickly now."

"That's good news," I say, though the words taste cautious.

He shrugs, leaning against the counter. "Good news till it isn't. They'll want tidy statements for the Bureau and the judge both. I'll handle the liaison; you keep her steady."

I glance up the stairs to where Mharie's still asleep, door cracked just enough to show the lamp glow. "She's steady enough to keep us both upright."

Brandon's grin edges tired. "No argument there." He finishes the mug and sets it in the sink. "I'm gonna drive into town drop the new photos with Mick, grab more printer ink. You need anything?"

"Just come back in one piece," I tell him.

He salutes lazily and steps back into the cold. The door closes, the house exhales, and I'm alone with the kettle's sigh. The quiet doesn't sit right, so I give it something to do. I clear a stack of old mail off Henry's roll-top desk the one that's been catching dust in the corner since we boxed up the last of his things. I never went through it proper, felt like crossing a line without her say-so. Beneath a folder of receipts, I find a false bottom I didn't know was there. Inside is a single yellowed envelope, sealed but soft with years.

Elspeth Campbell written in Henry's hand.

I sit before I realize I'm sitting. The kettle clicks off, but I don't move to pour. I slit the flap clean and unfold the paper that smells faintly of cedar and lamp oil.

January 14, 1987

Elspeth,

Texas is louder than I promised, but the sky earns the noise. I think you'd like it here the way dawn starts low and climbs like it's tasting its own courage. The porch needs painting, the fences lean like old men, and the barn roof sighs when it rains, but it's honest work and it's mine. I mean for it to be yours too, if you'll let it.

Tell Mharie she's welcome anytime she's ready. No rush on that. Teenagers have their own country to defend, and I've no wish to steal her from it before she's done.

The ground here keeps what you give it. I'd like to believe people can too.

H.

The paper trembles slightly though my hands are steady. I read it twice, three times, the way you read a map, even when you already know the way.

The doorframe creaks. "Patrick?"

She stands there, hair loose, sweater sliding off one shoulder, eyes still soft from sleep. "What're you reading?"

I hold out the letter. "Something your stepdad meant you to find, maybe."

She takes it carefully as a relic. The handwriting makes her mouth tremble before she finds any words. "Elspeth," she murmurs. "My mam."

She perches on the arm of the chair, the letter open between us. "She came after Christmas that year," she says quietly. "Gran was still weak, but she wanted Mam to go said she'd earned something bigger than the rain and the heather. They planned for me to follow once school was finished." Her smile is small, tired. "I told them both I needed to stay. I thought it'd only be for a year."

"You stayed for your gran?"

"I stayed because leaving felt like splitting the map in half. Mam had Henry, and I had her and both places felt like home." She presses her thumb to his name, gently. "He kept a place ready anyway."

"That's what love is," I say quietly. "Keeping the gate open, even when you're not sure who'll walk through."

Her eyes glisten, but she doesn't look away. "She used to write me about the land here. Said it had a hum under the soil. Maybe she meant him."

"Maybe she meant both."

She folds the letter once, then again, as if tucking both of them safely inside the years. "Maybe that's why he built this place the way he did. For whoever decided to stay."

I touch her wrist, light, grounding. "And you did."

"Aye." A small smile. "Eventually."

By midday, the wind kicks up, carrying a rattle of gravel from the road. When tires crunch the lane, I step out onto the porch.

A familiar rental car idles by the gate. He doesn't come past the chain, just stands outside it like he's learned the rules. The reporter, the one Dougal chased off, stands there clutching an apple and a notepad like a peace offering. His camera dangles at his side.

I walk halfway down the path, stopping where the fence throws its shadow. "You lost again?"

He clears his throat. "Mr. Williams. Ms. Campbell. I wanted to apologize for the last time. I well may have misread the cow's intentions."

I glance toward the pasture. Dougal stares back, cud working in lazy contempt. "He's philosophical, not malicious."

The man swallows. "Right." He extends the apple through the rails like a diplomat offering tribute. Dougal ambles closer, stretches his shaggy neck, and plucks it neatly from the man's palm. The crunch echoes down the lane.

For one blissful second, peace reigns then Dougal lifts his massive head, eyes narrowing as he sniffs at the reporter's coat. The man pats his pockets nervously. Dougal takes this as confirmation that more treasure exists and starts a slow, investigative frisk of the fence line.

"Ah he's friendly, right?" the reporter asks, edging backward.

"Friendly," I say. "Persistent is the word you're looking for."

"Understood." He retreats a step as Dougal snorts, disappointed by the lack of second offerings. "Look, I'm not here to stir trouble. Folks in town are saying federal agents were in court this week. I'm writing about corruption in small-county systems. Editors changed the angle after what happened at the courthouse," he adds, looking uncomfortable. "Human interest doesn't cut it when federal badges show up. Thought maybe you'd like your side told right."

Mharie steps out beside me before I can answer. She's in Henry's old coat, chin high, that look she gets when she's decided truth's worth more than comfort.

"Our side's simple," she says. "We kept records. We stayed honest. We didna scare easy."

He scribbles, glancing up. "Mind if I quote that?"

"Print it exactly as said," she replies. "Accent and all."

His smile wobbles. "Fair enough." He tips his camera toward Dougal. "Mind if I "

Dougal bellows once, sharp and triumphant, the sound of a creature who's just remembered the existence of apples. The crow on the fence takes off in protest.

"Maybe best not," I suggest.

"Right," the reporter says quickly. "Appreciate your time." He backs the car, relief nearly visible, and drives off in a spray of gravel.

I shake my head. "Dougal's going to think that's a game."

"He can play philosopher and sentry both," she says, laughing softly. "Seems he's good at both."

Late afternoon settles cold and flat across the yard. I find her inside, at the kitchen table with Henry's letter spread beside her notebook. She's tracing one line with her finger, the one that reads: *The ground here keeps what you give it.*

"He loved her fiercely," she says without looking up. "Didn't he?"

"Yes. In the same way he loved this place."

"And maybe the same way I'm learning to."

"That's not a bad inheritance."

She folds the letter once more and sets it on the mantel beside the binder. Paper and proof. Past and present. Both matter.

When the lamps are lit, Brandon returns, boots muddy, grin sharp with the weather. "Reporter was back?" he asks.

"Yep," I say. "Left wiser than he came."

"Good," he says. "I'll take that as progress." He pours himself coffee, nods toward the mantel. "Find something?"

"Henry's letter to Elspeth," I tell him.

Brandon studies the envelope a moment, not recognizing the name but respectful all the same, something in his expression softening under the weight of Henry's handwriting. "Seems he had a way of planning ahead."

"He did," I agree. "Even for things he couldn't see."

Outside the wind pushes around the eaves, the kind that promises colder nights and clearer mornings. Dougal's lowing drifts through it like an anchor.

Mharie stands beside me at the window, shoulder against mine. "Thirty-nine days," she murmurs.

"Thirty-nine," I echo.

The hinge on the gate sings once against the gust, honest and defiant. The sound hits clean. Like something finally shifting our way.

Chapter Thirty-Six

Mharie

The woodsmoke reaches me before the light does, the sharp kind that warns rather than comforts. I wake all at once, the way you do when your body has been listening on your behalf. The stove didna fail she only sulked. A handful of kindling, a coaxing breath, and the fire remembers itself. I set the kettle and stand in the pale not-morning, hands around a mug that isn't yet full, telling my bones we're still here.

Boots thump on the porch. The door creaks. Brandon slips in with the cold braided to his coat, breath fogging like he's dragged the morning in behind him.

"Perimeter's quiet," he says, stamping once. "One fox. Two crows are conducting a board meeting."

Patrick pours him coffee black, brutal. I wait for the kettle's mercy. "Anything else?" I ask.

"Only more good news." He lifts the mug, eyes closing like the heat reaches something wiring-deep. "Mick texted Austin's pushing the last of the paperwork. Could move fast now."

Patrick nods, cautious by habit. "Fast's fine so long as it's clean."

"It'll be clean." Brandon sets the mug aside and reaches for his truck keys, then thinks better and pockets them again. "You two should come in with me show your faces. Show Piper Falls who it's rooting for."

"Ye're recruiting us for a parade?" I say, half smiling.

"A parade of scones," he says solemnly. "Rosa's café."

The kettle clicks. I pour. We drink the way people do when something larger than thirst gets met for a minute. By the time we hit the road, frost is melting into tiny rivers across the hood and the sun's finally decided to report for duty.

Piper Falls in daylight looks like it always has determined to be kind. The café windows fog with warmth and the drunk-with-butter smell of something griddled. Rosa Martinez sees us coming and lifts the latch before we can touch it.

"Look at you three," she says, her smile half-mischief, half-mercy. "Heroes of bureaucratic romance. Get in before the biscuits lose their will to live."

"Morning, Rosa," Patrick says, the corners of his mouth easing. He's taller in here somehow. Men get that way when home recognizes them.

She steers us to the corner booth near the pie case where the sun lands. "Tea for you," she tells me, already fetching the pot, "coffee for the brooding pair. And don't argue Henry used to drink both, and I never let him pick or he'd never sit."

The name lands softly but whole. "Aye," I say. "Thank you."

The room runs on conversation more than electricity. Dale from the feed store raises two fingers in a salute that doesn't make a fuss but manages to mean everything. Mrs. Ortiz is at the counter, no grandkids in tow this morning just a stack of papers she's grading between sips. She tilts her chin toward me, that look she wears when she's decided on your behalf that you'll make it.

Rosa sets down the pot and three mugs like communion. "Scones with jam," she announces, as if the county passed a law. "And if any reporter puts one toe over my threshold to bother you while you eat, I will escort them out by the ear like my auntie used to do to my cousin Marco."

Brandon snorts. "I would pay to see that."

"You couldn't afford the ticket," she says, and kisses the top of my hair before skating away.

It's impossible not to breathe easier in a room like this walls that remember your footsteps, steam that says you belong to a human invention called comfort. Patrick's knee bumps mine under the table, small alignment, no fanfare.

"Word's out?" he asks, looking toward the window where the world drifts by with its errands, pretending not to watch us.

"Everyone knows," I say. "They also know how to behave." I nod toward the lone camera at the far table. The young man wearing it looks anywhere but this direction, cheeks red with trying to be good. "Mostly."

The scones arrive golden, disrespectfully perfect. The jam is the color of late summer and stubborn memory. For a minute, we eat like even judges have to step aside for butter.

The door opens on a bell that's seen better days. Sheriff Cantu ducks under the wreath someone hung too early for a holiday that's already passed and tips his hat. "Morning," he says to the room, which answers back as a single animal. He stops by our booth with a stance so non-threatening I could lean against it. "Mharie." A nod that carries years. "Patrick." Another, measuring. "And you must be Brandon." His eyes flicker, taking measure, finding no cause to write down. "Heard you had federal company in our house this week."

"We did," I say. "Came in with their pens uncapped."

"Good." He nods once. "If you get bothered at the gate again, you call dispatch. We like a posted sign; we love enforcement."

"Thanks, Sheriff," Patrick says.

Cantu looks like a man compiling a list of who in his town needs guarding. "Mrs. Ortiz asked me to tell you the kids are collecting canned goods for the winter drive. She says she'll send some of the older ones to help stack hay if you'll let them sign it as community service."

My mouth goes round with a laugh I didna expect. "Tell her I'll sign whatever they need so long as they keep their boots on and don't try to pet Dougal without an escort."

"Now that's a sermon," he says, touching his brim again. "Enjoy your tea."

When he leaves, the room exhales and moves again.

Brandon leans back, stretching the tension out of his shoulders. "You see that?" he says. "That right there is why you show up and eat where everyone can see. The town remembers whose side it's on."

"Was it ever in doubt?" Patrick asks, eyebrow up.

Brandon points his chin at me, but his voice gentles. "Sometimes the one bleeding doubts it first."

I pretend not to hear, which is to say I hear too well. Brandon drains his mug and pushes back from the booth. "I'm gonna run to Mick's and then the clerk's keep the cart from losing a wheel."

He looks at me over the rim of his grin. "You want anything from town? Nails? Gossip?"

"Don't come back empty-handed or hungry," I tell him. "Rosa'll never forgive us."

He taps the table twice superstition or punctuation, I can't tell and ghosts out.

For a few minutes, it's only us and the low hum of the place. Patrick watches me the way men do when they know you better than they should. "How's your tea?" he asks finally, voice careful and ordinary at the same time.

"Less wild than last night," I admit. "No' calm. Just... bearing me up." I lift my chin toward the door. "They do that."

"They do," he says. Then, without ceremony, he reaches under the table and takes my hand. We don't make a tableau of it; we are just touching. Heat travels skin to skin, and nowhere else has to patrol that border.

We attempt to pay; Rosa shoves my money back with the ferocity of a saint and flicks her towel at Patrick when he tries a different angle. "Henry fed the volunteer firemen for a year out of his own pocket," she says, voice gentling. "Let me feed his girl for a day."

I nod because I need it more than I can admit. "Thank you," I say, worn words with fresh edges.

Outside, the sun shines like a promise. We stand at the top of the steps a moment longer than necessary, letting the street's rhythm settle into our bones. Trucks pass. Someone's dog drags its human into a snowbank left in the shade of the feed store awning. The wind carries cedar and the metallic tang of cold that wants to be something else by afternoon.

"We can pick up the prints for Mick," Patrick says, glancing toward Main, where the little office supply sits like a stubborn cousin to the courthouse. "Save Brandon a trip back."

"Aye," I say. "And maybe a packet of those fancy paper clips that keep things from running off the edges."

We make an errand of it, which is to say we let ourselves be known. At the copy shop, Bev counts the pages twice, then adds a free ream to the stack without meeting my eye, as if generosity prefers to be unobserved. At the bakery, we buy two star cookies iced with shaky geometry because I say we should and Patrick never argues with sugar.

By the time we point the truck back toward home, the day's stretched thin enough for thoughts to move freely inside it. The fields lie pale and honest. Fenceposts tick by like a metronome. A hawk makes a dark note over the creek and writes its own music onto the air.

The gate hinge sings when we swing through. Dougal bawls like a king whose court has been late returning with news. We oblige him with hay and a scratch in the place between his horn and his ear where even philosophers go soft.

Inside, the house has kept our heat the way good rooms do when they've decided to love you back. I set Rosa's leftover scones on the counter and make tea the way Henry taught me don't wake what you don't need and Patrick lays the packet from Bev next to the binder like an offering. For a minute, we just stand and listen. The stove ticks. The wind nudges the eaves. The cameras blink their patient little eyes.

"Tomorrow," he says finally, "that's when the tide turns."

"And the Bureau?" I ask.

He taps the packet. "Moving."

It lands just under my ribs, that word moving like a small boat you thought was tied for good has nudged the dock and asked to be taken out. I don't cry. I don't need to. The light climbs the far wall an inch at a time, and for the first time in a long run of days, the quiet feels less like a test and more like a promise the world intends to keep.

Chapter Thirty-Seven

Patrick

The judge's gavel cracks once clean, final, a gunshot dressed as order. Every person in County Courtroom Two jumps then settles into the hush that only the judge can command. Mick stands three feet ahead, framed by the window's thin light. His voice is even, but I can hear the fatigue hiding under it, the kind that shows how hard this fight has been on everyone. "Your Honor, we seek relief from judgment on the grounds of fraud upon the court."

Each word lands like a grenade in the room.

Beside me, Mharie sits so still she might have been carved of stone chin high, shoulders square, hands laced tight enough to leave half-moons in her palms. Her coat smells faintly of peppermint and courage. Behind us, half of Piper Falls has come pretending to be neutral observers. I count Dale from the feed store, Mrs. Ortiz with her grading papers, Sheriff Cantu leaning against the wall pretending he's here for "security." Even the air feels like it's leaning forward.

At the defense table, Wendell's chair is empty cowardice posing as travel. His lawyer sweats through a suit that's trying too hard.

Federal Agents Hall and Morales sit in the front row, spines straight, hands folded. Their presence hums like static silent, but everyone knows it's there.

Judge Harlan rubs the bridge of his nose, eyes steady on Mick. "Fraud upon the court," he repeats. "That's a heavy phrase, Counselor. You prepared to prove it?"

"Yes, Your Honor," Mick says, and the way he says it makes the whole room lean forward.

He moves through the exhibits the way a craftsman builds a barn beam by beam. "Exhibit A: wire transfers to a family LLC registered to the previous judge's nephew's business.

Exhibit B: golf-trip invoices overlapping with weekends preceding rulings favorable to Mr. Sutton.

Exhibit C: photographs and sworn statements establishing contact between Mr. Sutton and the presiding judge outside lawful channels."

Papers whisper, boots scuff, someone coughs and immediately regrets it.

Harlan turns toward the agents. "And these documents are in federal custody?"

Hall rises. Her voice could cut glass. "Yes, Your Honor. All evidence has been verified. The Bureau has opened a parallel ethics investigation."

The defense lawyer clears his throat. "Your Honor, my client is ah temporarily unavailable to appear."

"Unavailable," Harlan repeats, tasting the word. "Or avoiding process?"

"Unavailable, Your Honor."

"Duly noted." His tone makes clear what he thinks of that.

Mick flips a page, slow and deliberate. "The record tells the same story this county's whispered for years," he says. "Today the story has ink."

The lawyer finds a scrap of defiance. "These payments could easily be charitable donations, golf-club dues small-town connections taken out of context."

"And yet," Mick answers, mild as rain, "when a man wins land he didn't earn and the judge who signs the order vacations in a condo paid for by that same man's shell company, the county's fondness for golf becomes relevant."

A laugh ripples through the benches before Cantu lifts one finger and the sound dies. The judge lets the quiet stretch till it turns heavy again.

"Fraud upon the court is a severe finding," Harlan says.

"So is stripping a woman of her home with a gavel bought by someone else's wallet," Mick replies.

That lands like thunder in the glen.

The judge studies the exhibits for so long I am worried he forgot we were there at all. Then he exhales.

"Accordingly," he says, voice slow and careful, "the prior order is vacated in its entirety. The grant of standing to Mr. Sutton is set aside. The directive that Ms. Campbell vacate the premises within forty-five days is null. Possession is restored pending further proceedings. This matter is referred to the state judicial-conduct commission and to federal authorities for coordination."

For a heartbeat, time stalls. Then sound returns in pieces someone gasps, another laughs, a chair leg scrapes.

Judge Harlan looks straight at her. "Ms. Campbell," he says, gentler now, "you did the work. The court recognizes that."

She nods once. "Aye."

He raps the gavel again. "We're adjourned."

The spell breaks. People rise carefully, as though the floor might shift if they move too fast. Mrs. Ortiz catches Mharie's hand; Dale gives a subtle salute. Cantu's nod could hold a parade if he wanted it to.

Hall and Morales gather their folders, exchange quick words with Mick follow-up interviews, Austin timeline. Wendell's lawyer bolts through a side door clutching his briefcase like someone might accost him.

Reporters swarm the aisle, voices tangling. "Ms. Campbell, how does it feel?"

Hall turns her badge just enough for the light to catch, and the whole crowd backs up like a herd meeting an electric fence.

I rest my hand at the small of Mharie's back. "Breathe," I whisper.

"I am," she says, though her voice shakes like she's still testing the word. "For the first time in weeks."

We step into air sharp enough to sting. The sky's winter-clean; sunlight cuts off the courthouse columns like a blade.

Brandon's waiting at the bottom of the steps, hands shoved into his jacket pockets, grin fierce. "Would you look at that," he says. "I came down here hoping for justice, and damned if we didn't find some."

"You look like a man who bet right," I tell him.

"Family's the only book I keep balanced." He claps my shoulder. "Austin's got their teeth in it now. Morales says the judge's nephew just remembered what conflict of interest means. Should be an interesting week."

Hall joins us, coat buttoned to her chin. "You did what needed doing," she says.

"I had help," Mharie answers.

Hall's mouth lifts at one corner. "The good kind." She and Morales disappear into a government sedan that hums away like quiet authority.

Rosa appears next, wrapped in her red coat, breath puffing clouds. She shoves a warm paper sack against my chest. "Butter rolls," she says. "Victory needs carbs. Don't argue. You two eat something that didn't come out of a jar."

Mharie blinks fast, smile fighting tears. "Thank ye."

Sheriff Cantu pauses halfway down the stairs. "Ms. Campbell," he says, voice warm. "Good to know that Highland Homestead sign's staying right where it belongs."

Her smile flickers but holds. "Maybe I'll give it a fresh coat of paint."

"Do that," he says, tipping his hat. "Let the county see it shine again."

The truck smells like coffee grounds and paper when we climb in. I start the engine, but we don't pull away right off. We just sit, letting the heater rattle and the adrenaline drain.

She watches the courthouse through the windshield, lips parted like she's still catching up. "It's done," she whispers.

"It's turning," I say. "Done comes later."

The drive home feels shorter than it has in weeks. Piper Falls hums along the roadside feed store bell clanging, kids skating on the patch of frozen puddle outside the library, Rosa's café window fogged and glowing gold. When people spot the truck, they raise hands without ceremony. You can feel the town choosing sides again.

At the bakery, a sign in the window reads *Fresh Bread, Honest Work,* and I swear someone did that on purpose.

Mharie sees it too. "Henry would've liked that."

"He would've framed it," I say.

The rest of the ride runs quiet. Snowmelt flashes silver on the blacktop; the fields lie open and waiting.

When we turn up the lane, the gate hinge sings its crooked song, same as ever but sweeter. Dougal bawls from the pasture, galloping that slow, ridiculous gallop until he stops at the fence.

"There he is," I say.

"There we are," she answers.

She feeds him the last apple from the dash. He crunches it with the reverence of a king accepting tribute.

Inside, the house smells like woodsmoke and a future that might stick. I drop Rosa's bag on the counter. Mharie hangs her coat by the door, fingers lingering on the hook like she's testing whether she can finally let go of the weight she's been carrying.

The binder waits on the mantel. It looks smaller today, ordinary. Evidence has become history.

She leans against me, shoulder to shoulder. "What happens now?"

"Now we keep receipts," I say. "And we live."

Her smile finds me without looking. "That'll do."

Outside the wind pushes once against the porch and then settles, satisfied. The hinge on the gate sings again clear, defiant, right.

I rest my hand over hers. For the first time since this started, the silence in this house isn't waiting for bad news. It's just waiting for morning.

Chapter Thirty-Eight

Mharie

I wake up in the morning and lie there for a moment. For the first time since I can remember, the peace I feel isn't temporary. The house is filled with the kind of silence that used to mean waiting for bad news, now it just feels... full. I lie there another minute, listening to Patrick move somewhere below bootsteps, the creak of a hinge, the deep rumble of Dougal scolding the world outside.

I walk downstairs and through the kitchen. When I reach the porch, the air bites, clean and sharp. Patrick's out by the fence, sleeves rolled, breath clouding the dawn. Dougal lumbers beside him, snorting steam, as if they're conspiring about fence lines and eternity.

He looks up when he hears me. "Tea's nearly on," he calls. "But I thought you'd want to see this first."

On the porch rail sits a long, canvas-wrapped board tied with twine. The kind of thing a man handles carefully, like he might remember.

"What is it?" I ask.

"Something that belongs home."

He kneels, unties the knots, and peels the canvas back.

HIGHLAND HOMESTEAD

Henry & Elspeth Sutton

Mharie Campbell

The words shine black against cream, letters carved deep enough to last another lifetime. The smell of paint hits first sharp, honest, new. Then the weight of it does.

My throat closes around the sight. "Patrick..."

"Rosa found it," he says. "After the flood, Henry donated some of the old signs to the church. She said she couldn't bear to throw this one out. I cleaned it up. Added what was missing."

I trace the curve of my name with a fingertip. The wood's warm from the morning light. "Ye didna have to."

"I wanted to. Henry built this place for his family. I just... finished the sentence."

Something inside me unwinds. The ache that's lived under my ribs for too long loosens its hold.

"Help me hang it?" he asks.

We carry it together to the gate, where the old Highland Homestead sign still hangs, faded, weather-beaten, Henry's letters nearly lost to sun and storm. Patrick lifts it carefully off its rusted screws, sets it aside like it's something alive. The post gives a little under the first nail of the new sign, soft from years of weather, then steadies as Patrick drives the hammer home. The sound rings out across the field. steady, final, true.

When he's done, he steps back, resting his hands on his hips. "There. Looks like it was always meant to be here."

Dougal ambles up from the pasture, eyes the sign, and lets out a low bellow that vibrates in my chest.

"Approval," Patrick says. "Or protest. Hard to tell with him."

"Call it approval," I say, laughing. "Feels better that way."

He grins. The morning light hits his face, and something in my chest stumbles.

He turns toward me, serious now. "You asked what happens next."

"Aye?"

He reaches into his coat pocket and pulls out the small box I thought he'd given up. The same ring, same shape, but everything around it is different.

"I asked you before because I wanted to do anything I could to help you," he says. "Because the land was in trouble, and I didn't know another way to help. I don't want to pretend anymore. I want to build something that doesn't need rescuing. Something that is ours."

My breath fogs between us. "Patrick "

"I'm asking again," he cuts in, voice quiet but sure. "Not for Henry. Not for paperwork. Just for you."

"I thought ye'd leave," I whisper. "Once it was done."

He shakes his head. "I called Adam this morning. Told him home's got a name now."

"And what did he say?"

"He said I'd be an idiot not to fight for the love of my life."

The laugh breaks halfway into a sob. "Then he's a wise man."

He steps closer, close enough that his breath warms my cheek. "So I'll ask once more will you marry me, Mharie Campbell? Because you want to."

I look at the ring, then at him, and somewhere between the two I find the answer I've been living toward. "Aye," I say, voice shaking. "Because I want to."

Patrick slips the ring onto my finger, and the world rearranges itself around that tiny circle of silver.

Dougal bellows again, startling a crow from the fencepost.

Patrick laughs. "That settles it. Official witness."

I can't help but laugh, "Rosa will want proof of signature."

Patrick knocks into my shoulder lightly, "She can officiate. Dougal can carry the bouquet."

I laugh until my ribs ache, and it feels like coming back to myself.

Inside, the house smells like woodsmoke and new beginnings. Patrick sets the kettle on while I hang our coats by the door. The binder sits on the mantel, closed, unneeded.

He pours tea into Henry's old, chipped mugs. "Tradition," he says.

We sit side by side on the worn sofa, knees brushing. The fire snaps and sighs. "Folk'll expect a wedding now," I tell him.

"They'd riot if we didn't."

"I always wanted a June wedding," I admit. "Before the Texas heat starts proper, when the honeysuckle's taking over the fencelines."

He smiles into his cup. "Then June it is. Big or small?"

"Small."

"Dougal?"

"He'll wear a bow."

"He will love it."

The laughter feels earned.

He sets his mug down and turns toward me fully. "You know, for all the noise we made getting here, it's the quiet that gets me. This house doesn't feel lonely anymore."

I nod. "Because it isn't."

We go out again just before dusk. The sky's the color of a penny held to flame, the air cold enough to sharpen breath. Frost clings to the new sign, glittering where the paint hasn't quite dried.

Patrick drapes an arm around my shoulders. I rest my head against him, watching the names catch the last light. "Keep the gate," I whisper.

He squeezes my hand. "Always."

Dougal shifts nearby, content, the steady sound of him chewing grass like punctuation to everything we've said. The wind moves through the oaks with a sigh that sounds almost human almost grateful.

Later, when the lamps are low and the stove's ticking itself to sleep, I find him by the window, looking out toward the pasture.

"What are ye thinking?" I ask.

"That I don't deserve this much peace," he says softly. "But I'm going to learn how to live with it anyway."

I cross the room, slide my arms around his waist from behind. "We both are."

He turns, kisses my forehead. "You look like you belong here."

"I finally do."

We climb the stairs together, still holding hands. At the landing, the firelight from below catches on the sign through the window **Henry & Elspeth Sutton. Mharie Campbell.** The glow makes it look like it's written in gold.

In our room, the quilts smell faintly of cedar and paint, of work done and promises kept. Patrick pulls me close, voice rough with tenderness.

"I meant what I said," he murmurs. "No more leaving."

"Good," I whisper. "Because I'd hunt ye down."

He laughs, that low sound that found its way into my bones. "Noted."

He tilts my chin up, kisses me once more slow and sure, the kind that doesn't need witnesses. When I wake sometime in the night, the wind's gentle against the windows, the world is finally still. The sign outside creaks once in the breeze, the hinge singing its small hymn of home. For the first time in years, I don't brace for the sound. I just listen.

The ground here keeps what you give it.

Henry was right.

And I'm finally ready to give it everything.

Chapter Thirty-Nine

Brandon

The wheels hit the tarmac, and I let out a breath that sounds like relief or exhaustion.

Hard to tell which one fits.

By the time I pick up my truck from long-term parking, the airport's already shedding another crowd. The sky's that winter kind of blue thin and tired but still trying. I toss my bag onto the passenger seat, turn the key, and the old engine catches like it missed me.

Guess that makes two of us. Two weeks in Texas. One courtroom, two dozen headaches, one miracle.

Patrick and Mharie.

If you'd told me a year ago I'd see Patrick Williams voluntarily settle down, I'd have bet the ranch against it. Now he's standing on land that finally belongs to the woman who matches him beat for beat. The man looks lighter. So does the ground under his boots. They earned it every inch of that homestead fought back until it found its rightful hands again. Watching them together felt like balance returning to the universe. Loud, stubborn balance with a Scottish accent and a cow for a referee.

I merge onto the highway toward Willow Glen, the kind of drive that's equal parts muscle memory and ghosts. The town settles in my chest long before the sign appears *Population 3,214*, though half of them still think the census is government spying.

Somewhere between mile markers, my mind drifts. I see Mharie looking at Patrick after the ruling steady, sure. No fireworks, no speeches. Just quiet certainty that home isn't land or papers; it's choosing someone over and over until the world believes you mean it. That kind of love used to sound like a myth.

Lately, I'm not so sure.

The mountains pull closer, low and familiar. My pulse slows with every mile. Willow Glen still smells faintly of rain, hay, and too much coffee, and even though I've been gone less than a month, it feels like years. I should head straight home unpack, check the barn, call Adam but my stomach growls before my conscience can argue. There's only one place that makes coffee strong enough to put hair on regret: Christiane's Diner.

Main Street still wears its Christmas lights, a little late, like the town can't quite let go. The diner glows from the corner window steam on the glass, neon humming, the sign flickering between *OPEN* and *PEN*. I park at the curb, kill the engine, and sit for a second. There's comfort in knowing what waits inside warmth, pie, and Adam pretending not to hover around his wife even though she's only been postpartum for about ten minutes and already back running the diner.

Christiane had the baby while I was gone a little girl, Susanne, after her mother. Word travels fast, even from halfway across the country. And knowing Christiane, she probably gave birth on Thursday and was back pouring coffee Friday morning. I reach for my phone to text before going in, but it beats me to it buzzing violently across the console.

Adam. Figures.

"Jesus, give me a minute," I mutter, answering as I step into the cold. "I just parked. What's your malfunction?"

"Brandon," Adam snaps. There's background noise clatter, voices, something that doesn't sound like peace. "Where are you?"

"Where do you think? Just landed. Heading into the diner. You sound like you swallowed a hornet's nest."

"Do not come "

Static cuts him off. A shuffle. Then his voice again low, tight, too late.

" to the diner."

I push open the door anyway. The bell above it gives its familiar off-key chime, and a wave of heat and cinnamon rolls out, covering the sound of conversation as it snaps to a stop.

And then I see her.

Laney Brooks.

She's standing by the counter, coat over her arm, hair shorter but still catching the light like it remembers how. The years haven't changed that look she gets before she bolts chin high, eyes wide, heartbreak hidden behind manners.

I stop dead. The world tilts.

"Laney?" Her name comes out rough, like it had to fight through memory.

She freezes mid-step. Color drains from her face then rushes back. "Brandon," she breathes. We stare at each other long enough for the clock above the register to tick three times. Then my phone, still in my hand, buzzes again, and Adam's voice fills the silence, the sound of a man resigned to fate.

"Well," he mutters, loud enough for the nearest tables, "fuck."

The air shifts, like somebody opened a door to the past. Christiane, bless her, senses the explosion and pretends it isn't happening. She wipes an already spotless counter, humming under her breath like the diner's structural integrity depends on it.

Laney looks everywhere but at me. Then she does. Her gaze hits straight through me ten years compressed into one impossible second. We weren't kids the last time I saw her. Old enough to break each other clean through.

"Hi," she says, voice tight.

"Hi." Brilliant, Brandon. Pulitzer-winning dialogue.

Her hands clutch the strap of her bag like it's keeping her upright. "I didn't know you were "

"Back?"

"Here."

"Well," I say slowly, "apparently neither did Adam."

From the booth near the window, Adam groans into his palm. "I told you not to come."

"Yeah, maybe next time start with why."

He exhales like a man praying for teleportation. "Because she came back yesterday."

Laney flinches at *she*. I'm not sure which of us stops breathing first.

Christiane breaks the spell. "If everyone's done giving the gossip mill a head start, sit down before I start selling tickets."

Laney mutters something about needing to go, but Christiane's already pouring her coffee like fate's on a timetable. Adam slides over, making room I don't want but can't refuse.

I sit. Because that's what you do in Willow Glen you face what never stopped mattering.

Laney lowers herself across from me, hands trembling as she takes the cup. The scent of cinnamon and cream fills the space between us sweet, sharp, familiar.

"So," Adam says finally, breaking the silence. "How was Texas?"

"Warm," I answer. "We won."

"Good. Because from the look on your faces, the weather's about to turn."

I glare. "Not helping."

"Wasn't trying to," he mutters.

Christiane slides by with her own question. "Patrick and Mharie?"

"They're good," I say. "She owns the place outright now. He's different. Happier." The silence that follows isn't comfortable yet but it's not lethal either. Outside, frost glints on Main Street; inside, the diner's hum returns one cautious clink at a time. People resume pretending they're not listening.

Laney finally meets my eyes. "You look the same."

I huff a laugh. "You don't."

"Good different or bad different?"

"Different, different," I say. "Like you finally stopped trying to fix the world before breakfast."

Her lips twitch. "That only lasted until lunch." Something real flickers recognition or just the ghost of it.

Adam clears his throat the universal signal for *I'm about to make things worse.* "So," he says. "Is this where I leave before someone throws pie?"

Christiane swats him with a towel. "You're not leaving me with them unsupervised."

"Good point," he says. "Then I'll just "

"Sit." He sits.

Laney looks between us, half amused, half ready to bolt. "I should go."

"Yeah," I say quietly. "You probably should."

The words taste like regret, but they're right. She nods once, stands, and adjusts the strap of her bag. "I didn't plan this far."

"Never did," I say. "Guess some things don't change."

Her mouth curves, soft and tired. "Maybe not all of them."

Outside, the wind picks up, rattling the sign against the door *Christiane's Diner: Open Early, Close Late, Never Empty.*

That's about right.

The bell jingles as she steps into the cold. I watch her cross the street, hair catching the light the same way it did back when I thought forever was real. Adam mutters something that sounds suspiciously like a prayer. Christiane refills my coffee without asking. For the first time in a long time, I don't know what happens next.

All I know is she's here.

And gone.

And somehow, that still changes everything.

Also by

The Wild Child Reckless Series

This is Growing Up

She was his best friend's little sister and completely off-limits—until one unforgettable night changed everything. Now Delilah is famous, engaged, and untouchable... but Alexander isn't giving up that easily. Because he had her once, and he's not letting her go again.

This is Meant to Be

She's promised to another. He's risking everything to keep her. Lillian was never supposed to fall for Jensen—but now that she has, neither of them is willing to let go, no matter how high the price.

This is Taking Chances

He shattered her heart once. Now he's back—not just to make amends, but to prove he's worthy of the family he never knew he had. A deaf drummer with a broken past. A single mother who swore she'd never look back. One love story that refuses to stay buried.

This is Starting Over**

She was the one girl he swore off limits. Now she's all grown up, in danger—and back under his protection.

This time, he's not sure he can walk away.

Foster, Inc. Novellas

Jack Frost, CEO

She's his assistant. He's her father's enemy. Pretending to be engaged might save his business deal, but when sparks turn into something real, Jack has to decide if falling for Maisie is worth the risk—or the scandal.

Willow Glen Series

From Feud to Forever*

She stole the land he spent twenty years trying to reclaim. He's determined to make her regret it—until their bickering turns into banter and the sparks start flying. In a small town full of gossip and grudge matches, Adam and Christiane are about to find out that the line between hate and love is thinner than a fence post.

A Highland Homestead Christmas**

Also part of the Piper Falls Christmas Collection

She came to Texas to settle her stepfather's estate. He only meant to stop by for a cow. By one fake engagement, a meddling town, and a feud-hungry uncle later, Mharie Campbell and Patrick Williams are knee-deep in Christmas chaos–and each other. In Piper Falls, where traditions fun deep and every secret sparks a rumor, they'll have to decide if what started as pretend is worth keeping for real.

Anything But Ordinary**

He likes life simple and quiet. She was the girl who once blew it wide open. Now Laney Brooks is back in Willow Glen—older, braver, and dragging a chaos-loving yellow lab straight into Brandon Williams's carefully ordered world. In a town where memories run deep and second chances don't come easy, these former sweethearts will have to decide if the love they lost is worth fighting for... or finally letting go.

Sons of Santoro Series

Tasting Sin-

Also part of the Sexy as Sin: Las Vegas World

She's the boss with everything to lose. He's the chef with nothing left to prove.

When a high-stakes sabotage threatens Sienna Moreau's Las Vegas hotel, she turns to the one man who infuriates and tempts her in equal measure—Luca Santoro. In a city built on secrets, desire becomes their sharpest weapon... but trusting each other might be the biggest gamble of all.

Monroe Strategic Capital Series

The Christmas Waffle*

He's a grumpy CEO with a plan for everything. She's the too-young, off-limits assistant who blows it all to hell with one unforgettable night—and one life-changing surprise. Now, with secrets, misunderstandings, and a baby on the line, they'll have to decide if their second chance is worth risking everything for.

*2025 $0.99 Preorder

** 2026 $0.99 Preorder

From the Author

Thank you for reading!!! If you have a moment please leave a review- they are so incredibly important to indie authors. I always loved reading, and now I have a separate love of writing. I hope you stick around and join me in this amazing adventure! I am always looking to connect! You can find me in the following places.

SmutTok Made Me Do It Facebook Group

Juliet McKinleys Book Nook

Sign Up for my newsletter here so that you never miss a beat, giveaway or sneak peek-

Newsletter   julietmckinley.myflodesk.com

TikTok   @JulieyMcKinleyAuthor

Instagram   @JulietMckinleyAuthor

Facebook   Juliet McKinley

* 9 7 9 8 9 8 9 5 1 7 3 5 0 *